Chestnut Gold

Patricia Leitch started riding when a friend persuaded her to go on a pony trekking holiday – and by the following summer she had her own Highland pony, Kirsty. She wrote her first book shortly after this and writing is now her full-time occupation, but she has also done all sorts of different jobs, including being a riding-school instructor, groom, teacher and librarian. She lives in Renfrewshire, Scotland, with a bearded collie called Meg.

Patricia Leitch

Chestnut Gold

An Original Armada

Chestnut Gold was first published in Armada in 1984
This impression 1988

Armada is an imprint of the
Children's Division, part of
the Collins Publishing Group,
8 Grafton Street, London W1X 3LA

Printed and bound in Great Britain by
William Collins Sons & Co. Ltd, Glasgow

CHAPTER ONE

From the high moors the dark figure of a man came striding down through the dawn silence towards Finmory House. The wind whipped his mane of blue-black hair about his gaunt face. His green eyes shone with an inward light like the depth of a wave pierced by the sun. As he made his way towards Finmory, he never lifted his gaze from the small, high window of the room where Jinny Manders lay asleep.

In her field beyond Finmory House, Shantih, Jinny's chestnut Arab, was standing in the corner closest to the moors. Although she could not see the approaching stranger she seemed to sense his presence and with lifted head, bright eyes and pricked ears she whinnied a welcome.

The man stopped at the edge of Finmory's grounds. He stood staring up at Jinny's window, standing without movement, so still that he might have been growing from the hillside. His black clothes seemed moulded to his long limbs and stooping back. The skin of his bony hands and face was dry and wrinkled. He waited while the sky grew clear, the first gulls screeched, and the rising disc of the sun swam upwards behind the mountains. But as the first rays of the sun cascaded over the moorland he turned away and went on towards Inverburgh, a moving shadow through the brightening morning.

No one saw him come or go. Only Shantih's bannering whinny and the drum beat of her hooves

7

as she galloped up and down her field, followed him over the hillside.

On the afternoon of the same day, Jinny Manders was sitting on the front steps of Finmory House. She was dressed in her new riding clothes and was watching the hands of her watch creep from four o'clock to half past. When the minute hand reached the half hour, then, at last, it would be time for her to saddle up Shantih and ride to meet the Hortons who were coming to camp at Finmory Bay. Jinny shook the watch irritably, held it up to her ear, but it hadn't stopped.

'Ten minutes more,' she told herself. 'Another ten minutes and then I can start.'

To set off too soon would be no use, for Jinny knew exactly where she wanted to meet the Hortons. She wanted to meet them where the road snaked down between the moorland to Glenbost village. Then she could watch their car coming towards her, giving her long delicious moments of anticipation – sweet and secret – not yet spoilt by the reality of Sue and her parents. Moments when she could see Pippen's trailer bouncing along behind the Hortons' car, and be able to imagine Pippen, self-contained and placid, eyes half closed as he endured the journey, and know that her dream of riding back to Finmory with Sue was about to happen.

'Sue,' thought Jinny with pleasure. 'Sue and Pippen.'

A year ago the Hortons had camped at Finmory Bay and Jinny had made friends with Sue, a girl of her own age who was as crazy about horses as Jinny herself. All summer Jinny had been waiting for the Hortons to come back. They had been on holiday in Greece but had planned to camp at Finmory for a fortnight when they came home from abroad. The fortnight had been changed to a week, and now, in the very last week of Jinny's summer holidays, they were coming. At last Jinny would have someone to ride with; someone to talk to about Shantih and know that they were really interested in what she was saying.

No one in Jinny's family was the least horsy. Two years ago the Manders had lived in Stopton, a city filled with metal noise and restless feet, driven by a constant vibration of fear. But now they lived in Finmory House, a stone house in the north-west of Scotland, that stood between wild moorland and Finmory Bay.

Jinny's father had been a probation officer in Stopton and was now a potter, so worried about making enough money to support his family that most of the time he only saw Shantih as an unnecessary expense. Jinny's mother listened to Jinny's endless horse madness because she loved Jinny, not because she was interested in horses. Mike was eleven, two years younger than Jinny. Although he rode Bramble, a black Highland pony borrowed from Miss Tuke's trekking centre, to school in Glenbost village, he was really only waiting for the time when he could trade in Bramble for a motorbike.

Petra, Jinny's sixteen-year-old sister was smart, noticeably clean and had crisp, brown, curly hair. Most of the time she read fashion magazines and practised the piano. She hardly ever rode. Often Jinny would stare at her sister, wondering what it would be like to be someone as tight and closed in as Petra, someone so certain about right and wrong, should and shouldn't; someone who only thought

9

about music exams, when there was a pure-bred, Arab mare in her family.

All through her summer holidays Jinny had been waiting for Sue to arrive and now, in another hour at the very most, there would be Sue. Sue and Pippen. Sue with her tales of her English Pony Club; who knew the correct way to do things; riding and jumping in the way she had been taught, not in a mad, uncontrolled frenzy of flying red hair, chestnut mane and intoxicating speed, which was the way Jinny rode Shantih.

The minute hand of Jinny's watch reached twenty-five past four. It was enough. Even if Jinny did have to wait for a few minutes it wouldn't be long enough for Shantih to get bored. Jinny sprang to her feet and raced over the rough grass of Finmory's lawns towards the loosebox where Shantih, groomed to perfection, was waiting.

Hearing her mistress's running footsteps Shantih whinnied impatiently, kicking at her box door with peevish fore hooves. When the Manders had first come to Finmory, the stables had been decaying outhouses but now they were a loosebox for Shantih, two stalls and a combined feed house and tack room.

Suddenly Jinny stopped in mid stride.

'Drat and double drat,' she muttered. 'Forgot my flippin' hat!'

For a moment she considered going on and riding without it. But only for a moment. Her parents, who didn't bother too much about what Jinny did on Shantih, were totally fixated on the fact that if Jinny was riding she had to wear a hard hat.

'Forgot my hat,' Jinny yelled to Shantih, and spinning round raced back to the house.

As Jinny grabbed her hat from the hall table the

phone, squatting black and toad-like, burbled into life. Jinny stared at it furiously. She hadn't time to answer it, couldn't be bothered. Not now. Jinny knew that everyone was out, except Petra who was having a bath. Letting the phone ring, Jinny stared hopefully up the broad staircase, wondering if Petra would come down to answer it.

Although having a bath in the afternoon with bath foam, body lotion and clouds of talc was one of Petra's favourite occupations, Jinny suspected that today Petra was probably sitting on the edge of the bath having a good cry. That morning Petra had heard that she had failed a music exam.

'First time for everything,' Jinny had said cheerfully, when Petra opened the envelope containing the incredible news and announced her failure.

'Really, Jinny,' her mother had said sharply. 'Don't be so cruel.'

'Well, she's bound to pass next time, aren't you, Petra?' Jinny had said, knowing that once she started sitting exams she was bound to fail, totally, completely, utterly, and that she had better make the most of what was likely to be Petra's one and only failure.

The phone rang on.

'Might be Sue,' Jinny thought suddenly and grabbed the receiver.

'Hallo,' she said. 'Jinny here,' and Petra, still fully dressed, came to the top of the stairs, her red eyes confirming Jinny's suspicions.

'Ah, Jinny! Good show! Just who I wanted,' boomed Miss Tuke's loudspeaker voice. 'Crisis here.'

Jinny imagined Miss Tuke's trekking centre burnt

11

to the ground, her Highland ponies fleeing across the hills, or Miss Tuke in plaster to the neck after some horrific accident.

'I am phoning you against my better judgement,' continued Miss Tuke.

'Who is it?' demanded Petra.

'For me,' Jinny told her, hand over the mouthpiece, thinking that it had nothing to do with Petra.

'Who?'

'Miss Tuke,' mouthed Jinny, expecting Petra to go back to her bathroom once she knew. But Petra didn't. She came down the stairs and sat on a step close enough to the phone to be able to catch some of Miss Tuke's conversation.

'So I must find someone to ride with us.'

'What's that? Sorry,' said Jinny, scowling at Petra to let her know that she had caused her to miss Miss Tuke's vital, crisis communication. 'To ride where? When?'

'For heaven's sake pay attention, girl. This is urgent. We're leaving Monday morning. Can you come?'

'Think I missed a bit,' said Jinny, not having the faintest idea what Miss Tuke was talking about. 'Could you tell me again?'

'Glory help me!' exclaimed Miss Tuke in exasperation. 'Having to depend on you. Now listen.'

Jinny wanted to tell her that it was all Petra's fault for interrupting, but decided not to, in case Miss Tuke lost her patience and put the phone down.

'I'm listening,' Jinny assured her.

'As I've already told you, my nephew Royce Bryden is a film director. He's making a series on

"The Horse" for ITV. Pretty big production. Coming over to film at Calmun – a day's ride from here. Hiring eight of my Highlands. Whole thing fixed up months ago. Six experienced trekkers ready to pay double for a Film and Trek week, which, plus the television fees, should have brought in a nice little bit extra. Phone call this lunchtime, Mr and Mrs Pennington and their two kids struck down with chickenpox. Leaves me with four ponies to be trekked to Calmun and no bods to sit on them. Could box them over, I suppose, but the other two trekkers are on their way here this very min. expecting a two day trek to Calmun. Bed and breakfast booked for Monday night. Calmun Hotel for the rest of the time, back here in one day. So how about it?'

'You mean ride with you? Me?' exclaimed Jinny, and for a second she was astride Shantih, leading two Highlands, riding over new country with the thought of filming ahead of her. 'But Sue's coming.'

'Even better. Thought it was this week the Hortons were camping. She can come too.'

'That would be absolutely super!'

'What?' demanded Petra from her stair. 'What would be super?'

'I'm sure she would love to come,' said Jinny, ignoring her sister. 'And Pippen is dead quiet. Sue will easily manage to lead a Highland from him.'

'Pippen? Do not tell me she is carting that animal all the way up here for one week? Can't bring him on the trek. You'll each have to ride a Highland and lead one. Got to get four ponies to Calmun.'

'Then we can't come,' stated Jinny. She had known it was too good to be true. 'Sue would have to ride Pippen and I would have to ride Shantih.'

13

'Nonsense,' snapped Miss Tuke.

'Definite,' said Jinny. 'But we could lead a Highland each.' Jinny heard Miss Tuke tutting irritably, then someone shouting to her.

'That's one of the trekkers arriving now,' said Miss Tuke. 'I suppose the wretched child will want to ride her own pony when they've dragged it up here.'

'And I MUST ride Shantih.'

'I could lead Juno as well as Misty. You could lead Bramble. Sue lead Heather. I'm riding Guizer. Fergus and McSporran for the trekkers. Still leaves Beech. What about that sister of yours? I'm desperate. Cannot rouse anyone at such short notice. She can ride, can't she?'

'Petra? Oh, she wouldn't want to come. I could lead Beech and Bramble.'

'Where wouldn't I want to go? How do you know I wouldn't want to go?' demanded Petra.

'Disaster,' said Miss Tuke, meaning Jinny leading two ponies from Shantih. 'Phone me when you've discussed it with Sue. Got to get it settled tonight.'

'We couldn't afford to pay,' Jinny said hurriedly, in case Miss Tuke was expecting her to pay double, when she most certainly couldn't even begin to afford to pay single pony-trekking rates.

'Film company is paying all expenses. Phone me back,' and Miss Tuke crashed the phone down.

'What does Miss Tuke want you to do?' Petra nagged. 'Why did you tell her I wouldn't want to go when you hadn't asked me?'

'It's trekking, so I knew you wouldn't be interested. Miss Tuke has to take eight ponies to Calmun to be filmed. She wants Sue and me to ride with her. Of course you don't want to come. You'd hate it.'

'To be filmed? You mean proper professional filming?'

'Got to go and meet Sue,' Jinny yelled, snatching up her hard hat and dashing out of the house.

'Hush your mouth, Jinny Manders,' she told herself as she ran towards the stables, for the thought of being filmed was exactly the sort of thing that would make Petra want to go on the trek with them.

Shantih exploded from the dark of her loosebox into the blare of sunlight. The afternoon spangled into myriad reflections of brilliance as Shantih – neck arched, wide eyes glistening – danced at the length of her reins. She trumpeted her vexation at being kept shut up in a box when the sands of the bay waited for the imprint of her galloping hooves, and the breeze, blowing down from the moors, whispered of freedom and space and speed.

'For goodness sake,' muttered Jinny impatiently, as Shantih reared up against the blue sky, a golden silhouette of heraldic mane and carven, delicate muzzle. 'Stand still, idiot horse. The Hortons are going to be coming up the drive at this rate.'

Jinny tightened Shantih's girth, threw the reins over the mare's head and, tugging down her stirrups, sprang lightly into the saddle. She turned Shantih's head towards the track that led to Mr MacKenzie's farm and rode her firmly in the direction of Glenbost.

Ken Dawson was digging in his kitchen garden as Jinny trotted past.

'Ken could have come with us,' Jinny thought, sitting tight in the saddle as Shantih flung herself across the track to avoid the terrors of a lurking paper bag. But Ken was going on holiday for a fortnight to stay with a community in the east of Scotland.

Ken lived with the Manders, working in the pottery with Mr Manders and in the vegetable garden he had created; growing enough fruit and vegetables to feed them all. When Jinny had discovered Shantih being ill-treated in a cruel circus, Ken had known how vital it was for Jinny to rescue her, and it was Ken who had saved Jinny's life when he had found her searching for Shantih during a blizzard. He understood the strange magic power of the Red Horse mural which the tinkers had painted, many years ago, on the wall of the room in Finmory which now belonged to Jinny. He was one of the very few people to whom Jinny ever showed her own drawings and paintings.

Jinny touched Shantih into a canter.

'Been great if Ken could have come with us,' she thought.

Mr MacKenzie, the old farmer who farmed the land around Finmory, was revving up his tractor in the farmyard. Shantih stopped dead at the noise.

'Get on with you! You know it's only a tractor,' growled Jinny, as Shantih reared, refusing to pass it.

'Please switch the engine off,' Jinny pleaded above the din.

'Och now, and I never noticed you, creeping up on that horse of yours.'

'That will be right,' said Jinny, forcing Shantih past the still juddering tractor. 'I'm late. Going to meet Sue.'

'Then it is late you are, all right. The Hortons are just after phoning me from the Glenbost shop. They will be here before you, if you hang about at the gossiping all day.'

Mr MacKenzie started up his tractor again and the noise blasted Shantih into a gallop. Jinny leant

16

forward, her hands low on Shantih's neck, guiding
her horse along the sheep-cropped turf at the side of
the road to Glenbost. After spending all day
grooming Shantih and dressing herself up to impress
Sue, Jinny couldn't bear the thought of the Hortons
reaching Finmory before she had ridden out to meet
them. She wanted Sue to unbox Pippen so that they
could ride home together.

The Manders' car came ponderously along the
road towards Jinny but she didn't slow Shantih
down.

'We've seen them,' Mike shouted from the back
window. 'Wait till you see Sue. You'll not know her!'

Jinny paid no attention to him. She galloped on,
her mind set on reaching the place where the road
stretched down to Glenbost before the Hortons did.
She held the thought of the empty road clear in her
mind's eye as she urged Shantih on.

They reached the rise in the ground and Jinny
brought Shantih to a halt. The road was empty. Only
two sheep wandered across it.

'Made it,' Jinny told Shantih, slipping to the
ground. 'You remember Pippen? Well, he'll be here
any second now.'

As if waiting for its cue, the Horton's sleek estate
car purred into sight, Pippen's trailer trundling
behind it.

Jinny hadn't seen Sue since Easter and now it was
the end of August. She wondered what Mike could
have meant when he had said that she wouldn't know
Sue. Of course she would know Sue. Feeling
suddenly nervous Jinny pushed back her long red
hair; tried to arrange her sharp-featured face into a
welcoming expression. She wished that she hadn't
dressed herself up, wished that she was wearing her

usual jeans and tee shirt. But it was too late to change anything now.

'Don't be so daft,' Jinny told herself. 'It's only Sue. Bet she'll be really keen to go on Miss Tuke's trek. Super pleased to see Shantih again.'

But Jinny's reassurances to herself were on the surface of her mind. She had woven so many imaginings into their meeting, that now it was about to happen, she was frozen into a sudden self-consciousness: could not think what she was going to say to Sue.

CHAPTER TWO

The Hortons' car stopped beside Jinny and Sue erupted from it.

'Jinny!' she yelled. 'At last! It's taken us forever to get here. Poor old Pippen must be set solid. How are you?'

Jinny stared speechless, for it *was* Sue – but wasn't Sue. The old Sue had not been exactly fat, more thickset and sturdy, like the cobby Pippen; this new Sue was tall and slender, seemed inches taller than the Sue Horton who had stayed with Jinny at Easter. Not only was her slimness new, but her hair, that had been trimmed in a more or less pudding-basin cut, was now professionally styled into soft waves and a fringe.

'You have changed. You look quite different,' gasped Jinny.

'I'm not. It's still me. Only less of me. Mum had this great thing against sugar. Absolutely banned from the house. Nothing sweet. And this is what happened. Nearly a stone and a half gone, just vanished. Pippen can jump miles higher now. You're looking pretty poshed up yourself.'

'Ken bought them for me for a cross-country event. I don't really wear them. Only put them on to show off.'

'And Shantih is looking fantastic.'

Sue stroked Shantih's sleek neck, scratched behind her ears and at the root of her mane, as Mr and Mrs Horton got out of the car.

When they had finished greeting Jinny, Mr Horton asked what she thought of his daughter.

Jinny thought it was a stupid, smug kind of question and couldn't think what to say.

'Quite a change in her,' Mr Horton insisted proudly.

'Into what?' Jinny thought, imagining Sue's hands changing into paws, or horns starting to grow from her head. She stared down at her feet, digging her nails into the palms of her hands to stop herself giggling.

'You'll be next,' said Mrs Horton. 'Get some of that mane cut off. Start to take an interest in yourself.'

'If I lost a stone and a half I wouldn't be here, and I'm getting a bit cut off my hair before I go back to school,' Jinny defended herself. It was one thing for her mother to nag about the length of her hair, but quite another for Mrs Horton to start on about it when she hadn't seen Jinny for a year.

'Saw your parents in Glenbost,' said Mr Horton. 'They asked us in for a cuppa before we start pitching the tent, so we'll see you at Finmory,' and to Jinny's dismay the Hortons started to get back into their car again.

Jinny stared helplessly. Surely Sue would want to ride back to Finmory with her. Riding to Finmory with Sue was so much part of Jinny's dream-meeting with the Hortons, she could hardly realise that it was in danger of not coming true.

'What's wrong?' asked Sue, and for a moment she was her old self again – straight, concerned, honest.

Jinny shrugged her shoulders, thought she would say nothing, let her dream sink back and be forgotten, but she had pumped too much energy into it. She had lived the ride back to Finmory over and over again; riding with Sue, telling her about Shantih.

'Thought we could ride back together . . .'

'Oh yes, of course,' said Sue, her enthusiasm lifting Jinny's spirits. 'Dad, could we unbox Pippen here, and I'll ride with Jinny?'

Rather unwillingly Mr Horton agreed, and in minutes Sue was backing Pippen down the ramp of the trailer. Jinny gasped in surprise when she saw the skewbald Pippen. Last summer Pippen's mane had stuck up like a shaving brush, now it fell in a neat, pulled fringe, lying correctly down one side of his neck.

'I managed to grow it at last,' said Sue, as Jinny clapped Pippen, and held out her palm for his lipping caress. 'Looks a lot better, doesn't it?'

'No. I liked it better the way it was last year,' stated Jinny, meaning not only Pippen but Sue as well.

'Don't you notice anything else different?' asked Sue, when the Hortons had driven out of sight and Sue and Jinny were riding together. 'About me?'

'Not really,' said Jinny, wanting to tell Sue about Miss Tuke's trek. 'I've noticed your hair and most of you having vanished.'

'My eyes,' said Sue.

'Contact lenses?' suggested Jinny.

'No! Course not. My eye make-up. When we were in Greece there was this girl on our tour and she showed me how to make up my eyes properly. Don't you think it makes a difference? I'll show you how to do it.'

'Yuk,' said Jinny. 'I don't want my eyes all clogged up. Dare say Petra would be quite interested. You can show her.'

'Sorry,' said Sue. 'It was only to show off. Same as your clothes.'

Jinny didn't think it was the same at all. How could eye make-up be the same as new jodhs, a tweed hacking jacket and black rubber riding boots?

For minutes they rode without speaking, each waiting for the other to speak first.

'Got any plans?' Sue asked, her voice stiff from having practised the words in her head.

'Miss Tuke has,' said Jinny and told Sue about the trek and the filming.

'Oh, we must go. I could easily lead a Highland from Pippen. He wouldn't mind a bit.'

'I've to phone Miss Tuke after I've discussed it with you. Do you know what she suggested? She suggested that Petra might like to come!' Jinny paused, waiting for Sue's shocked exclamation at such a nonsense. But Sue said nothing.

'Miss Tuke thought that Petra could ride a Highland all that way. Imagine Petra trekking!' Jinny continued, demanding Sue's agreement.

'Perhaps she would like to see the filming. Maybe she thinks she'll be discovered. This girl I was telling you about, the one I met in Greece, well she does modelling. Used to model teenage fashions but now she's hoping to break into the big time. She says she's going to take London by storm.'

As if her stomach were suddenly ice cold and heavy, Jinny felt it sink with disappointment. What had happened to Sue? Jinny wanted to tell her about Shantih, not listen to her talking about a fashion model; wanted her to agree how it would spoil everything if Petra were to come on the trek with them.

'You should have seen some of the fantastic clothes she wore,' said Sue.

22

'Shall we trot?' said Jinny, and not waiting for a reply she released Shantih into a battering trot.

Petra noticed Sue's eye make-up at once.

'Whoever did your eyes?' she asked, when the chorus of admiration in praise of Sue's new-found slimness had died away.

Jinny plonked herself down at the table where Manders and Hortons were drinking tea.

'Miss Tuke wants Sue and me to trek to Calmun with her, help her take her Highlands over to be filmed,' Jinny announced, reaching across the table for a scone. 'I've to phone her.'

Mrs Manders looked quickly at Petra.

'You don't need to,' said Petra. 'I phoned her. It's all arranged. I'm coming too, so you can ride Shantih and Sue can ride Pippen.'

'Oh no! No!' cried Jinny, her knife clattering to her plate. 'You can't come. You'll spoil everything.'

'Jinny,' warned her father.

'But she will. On at me all the time. Have I washed my neck? Are my nails clean? Checking up on what I'm doing. Where I am. Telling me how to ride Shantih, when she wouldn't even sit on her.'

'Too much,' said her father in the tone of voice with which Jinny never argued.

'She can't come,' Jinny muttered under her breath, lumping butter on to her scone. 'The trek is for Sue and me. Not Petra!'

'Don't go then,' said Ken, when, later in the evening, Jinny and Ken were alone in the kitchen.

'But I want to go. I just don't want Petra there.'

'She's going. You haven't any choice.'

'All spoilt,' sulked Jinny. 'All ruined. Polluted by Petra.'

When Jinny tried to complain about it to her

mother, Mrs Manders told her sharply not to be so childish; that it was just what Petra needed to take her mind off her failed music exam.

Mr Manders telephoned Miss Tuke himself, mainly to make sure that the trek wasn't going to cost anything and also to check up on her arrangements.

'Leave first thing Monday morning,' Miss Tuke told him. 'Monday night bed and breakfast at the Lillybank Guest House. Trek to Calmun. Spend two nights in the hotel there while Royce is filming the ponies, then back here in one day. Film company pays all expenses and a tidy little capitalist sum towards my feed bill.'

'Do they need a potter?' asked Mr Manders.

'Unfortunately not but you'll be bringing Petra over? Jinny and Sue will be riding?'

'Knew it,' said Mr Manders. 'Anything like this always involves me in driving people about and the price of petrol . . .'

'Good show,' interrupted Miss Tuke. 'See you when it suits.'

Jinny and Sue arrived at Miss Tuke's trekking centre shortly after six the next evening. Jinny had given up. She had stopped trying to talk to Sue about Shantih or Pippen and had spent the ride listening to her talking about clothes and make-up and the fantastic time she had had in Greece. Miss Tuke was standing in her doorway, looking out for them. Parked in her driveway was a scarlet sports car with orange leather upholstery.

'On the dot,' said Miss Tuke. 'Royce has arrived. Going to tell us something about his film. Wants the ponies to stampede over the moor or some such nonsense. I'll sort him out when we get there. Right, let's get your nags parked,' and Miss Tuke led the way round the side of her house to the stable yard.

'Bramble!' cried Jinny in delight, as Bramble came bustling across the paddock towards them. His dark eyes were bright under his knotted brows. He whiffled an uncertain welcome, then, sure that it really was Jinny and Shantih, he gave vent to a clarion blast of delight.

'Have missed you,' Jinny told him, scratching along his mane. 'You'll be back home soon but first you're going to be a film star. Well, a telly star. The whole world will see you.'

Bramble, nudging at Jinny's pocket, remained unimpressed by his future fame.

'Put your two in with Bramble and Heather,' Miss Tuke said when she had finished expressing her amazement at Sue's new shape.

'You're to lead Heather,' she told Sue, pointing to the white, Western Isles type Highland who was in the paddock with Bramble. We'll leave the four of them here for tonight. Get any nonsense out of their heads before we set off tomorrow.'

When they had watered and fed their horses Sue and Jinny turned them out into the paddock, but there was no nonsense. Shantih greeted Bramble with delight and in no time they were standing shoulder to shoulder, nibbling withers. Pippen rolled, struggled upright and began to tear at the grass. Heather blinked long-lashed eyes, pig-squealed at Pippen, but finding herself ignored went back to grazing.

'United Nations,' said Miss Tuke. 'Good show. Brought the others in for the night. Blasting off first thing in the morning. Want to see them?'

In the first of Miss Tuke's three looseboxes stood a

fifteen hand, dun Highland; massive as a tank, with an eel stripe and a black storm of mane and tail. Jinny recognised him as Guizer, the Highland Miss Tuke usually rode herself. A dapple-grey and a black stood in the other two boxes.

'I'm riding this fellow,' said Miss Tuke, clapping her broad, capable hand on Guizer's muscled shoulder. 'Leading these two. The grey is Misty. Broke her in myself. And the black is Juno. Only bought her this year.'

'All these ponies!' thought Jinny enviously. 'And all belonging to Miss Tuke!'

'Petra is to ride Beech,' said Miss Tuke, leading the way to where three Highlands stood in a row of stalls.

Beech was a bay pony of thirteen hands, showing a lot of white in his eyes and already thick coated for the coming winter.

'Never seen your sister on a horse. What's she like?'

'Oh, she can ride,' said Jinny, thinking that Petra's riding was like everything else about her. She could do almost everything but didn't really enjoy doing anything. She was always too busy worrying what other people were thinking about her. Even her piano playing was twisted up by exams; had no joy in it. 'She can ride, only she doesn't, not much.'

'This is Fergus,' said Miss Tuke, clapping the chestnut rump of the pony standing next to Beech. 'Mrs Brothwick, one of the trekkers, will be riding him. She sounded a very horsy little woman when she was letter-writing to me, but I'm afraid she is a very letter-writing little woman on a horse. Still, Fergus will keep an eye on her.'

'Brian Bain is the other trekker. Bit of a speed

merchant but McSporran will sort him out. Eh, McSporran?'

The mouse-dun McSporran turned a flat-boned, carthorse head at the sound of his name. Hay wisps hung from his rubbery lips, wrinkled eyelids lay heavily over sleepy eyes.

'Only eight. Answer to a trek leader's prayer. He'll go last no matter who you put on him,' and Jinny could have sworn that McSporran winked at Miss Tuke.

'That's it then. All set for tomorrow. Be a shock to their systems when we don't turn for home halfway through the day.'

Waiting for Miss Tuke to close the stable doors Jinny felt a zig-zag of excitement shiver along her spine. She stared up at the hillside, seeing the grazing shapes of Miss Tuke's other ponies. They were all to stay here, safe, secure on their familiar hill, while she would be on the trek, riding out into the unknown. Suddenly the trek to Calmun seemed like a trek to the Himalayas – anything might happen. If only Petra hadn't been coming too.

Jinny cast a last glance over the moors. A dark figure moved in the hill's shadows, arm uplifted as if trying to attract attention, but Jinny didn't see him. She checked on Shantih, then hurried after Sue and Miss Tuke.

CHAPTER THREE

They went into the house together, shedding jodh boots in the porch.

'Straight ahead,' said Miss Tuke. 'In through that door. I'll bring the coffee.'

The hallway was dark, its walls encrusted with rows of dusty rosettes. Jinny turned the door handle, knowing the room from meetings of Miss Tuke's Trekking Club. Firelight flickered beyond the opening door.

'At last! Where have you been? We've been waiting for you for hours!'

At the sound of her sister's voice Jinny's heart sank. It was as if, with Petra in the room, there wasn't enough air for Jinny to breathe; a tightness closed her in.

'*We* rode here,' she said. 'Not like some people who had to be brought by car.'

Jinny was aware of faces staring up at her, strangers already thinking of her as the difficult younger sister; but it was the only way Jinny could be when Petra was about.

Miss Tuke brought in a tray of mugs, coffee and biscuits, and while Petra poured out the coffee, being bright and social, Miss Tuke introduced Sue and Jinny.

Mrs Brothwick had cropped, steel-grey hair, beige skin and thick glasses. She held out her hand to Jinny, said how pleased she was to meet Petra's younger sister and how sure she was that they were all looking forward to seeing her wonderful Arab horse.

28

Brian looked a bit older than Petra. He was short and greasy and startled out of his chair to shake hands, sending cushions hurtling to the floor.

'And Royce Bryden,' introduced Miss Tuke. 'Our director.'

Miss Tuke's nephew uncoiled from the settee and, to Jinny's total amazement, kissed both Sue and herself.

'Wonderful to meet you. Auntie Tuke's been telling me how you've both stepped in at the last moment to ride her ponies to Calmun for us. Really do appreciate it. Really do.'

Still stunned by his embrace, Jinny blinked up at him. He was something new in her life. To kiss somebody you had never even seen before! The smell of his aftershave, his hard, cool cheek against hers were not at all what she was used to.

'Now you are Jinny, aren't you? Arab horse?'

Jinny nodded.

'"My beautiful! my beautiful! that standest meekly by,
With thy proudly-arched and glossy neck, and dark and fiery eye!
Fret not to roam the desert now with all thy winged speed:
I may not mount on thee again – thou'rt sold my Arab steed!"'

declaimed Royce.

A lump swelled in Jinny's throat. For a terrible moment she thought she was going to cry. The rest of the room swam out of focus. There was nothing but Royce – tall and slim, blond hair falling over blue eyes, clothes that looked as if they had come out of adverts in *Sunday Times* supplements. And here he was, standing in Miss Tuke's room talking to her; quoting one of her most favourite poems – 'The Arab's Farewell to His Steed' by the Honourable Mrs Norton. Jinny knew every word of it and here was Royce Bryden, a film director, quoting it to her.

'The last verse is the best,' said Royce.

'Oh yes!' agreed Jinny, and together the words of freedom tripped off their tongues.

> '"Who said that I had given you up? Who said that thou wert sold?
> 'Tis false! 'tis false! My Arab steed! I fling them back their gold!
> Thus, thus, I leap upon thy back and scour the distant plains!
> Away! who overtakes us now may claim thee for his pains!"

'Great stuff,' exclaimed Royce when they had reached the end. 'I can see we share a cultivated taste in horsy literature.'

'She's forever reciting that sort of thing,' said Petra. 'Quite mad.'

'All the best people are mad,' said Royce, putting his arm round Jinny's shoulders and crushing her to him. '"Thou shouldst go mad, blacksmith. I am impatient of all misery in others that is not mad." Read *Moby Dick*, no horses but what a whale.'

Jinny said she'd read bits of it because Ken liked it, but hadn't managed it all.

'You will,' Royce promised her.

'Here's your coffee,' said Petra, thrusting a mug at Jinny. 'Put your own milk in.'

Royce turned to Sue, asking her what form her hidden madness took.

'Right,' organised Miss Tuke, opening out a large scale Ordnance Survey map and spreading it out on the table. 'I'll show you our route. Forestry tracks to begin with, then open moorland, and we spend the first night here at Lillybank Guest House. Used to be a shooting lodge before the big estate was split up. Royce is leaving food for the nags there, and we're all booked in. Next day along an old drove track over the hills. This bit where we're right down between the mountains is called the Pass of the Horses, though what horses no one seems to know. That takes us to here.'

Miss Tuke's stubby finger suckered down on the map.

'We'll need to push on to arrive here in plenty of time, for the next bit's dicey. We've got to get down the hillside to Calmun.'

'Down there?' asked Petra anxiously. 'We've studied maps at school and those gradient lines are so close together it'll be a sheer drop.'

'We'll make it,' said Miss Tuke briskly. 'If the drovers could get their cattle down, we can get the ponies to do it.'

Jinny saw the corners of Petra's mouth tuck in, and her eyebrows slant, the way they did when she was nervous about something.

'Do not know what she bloomin' wanted to come for,' Jinny thought. 'She'll be scared stiff if we do have to ride down anywhere steep.'

'When I was looking at the map at home,' said Brian. 'Looking to see where we were going to be riding, like, our Babs' boyfriend, Dennis, was looking at it as well. He says we're close to what he

31

calls a ley line. He's into all that rubbish. Says one of the ancient ways was on these moors. Not old, like Victorian, but ancient, like Druids and Celts and even before that lot. Just thought I'd tell you for the laugh, like.'

'Royce,' said Miss Tuke impatiently. 'Over to you.'

Royce pushed back the fall of blond hair that slid over his eyes, sat forward on the settee talking intently.

'Well, it's to be a series in three parts. My original idea would have made a ten-hour epic covering every aspect of the horse. I've pruned it down to three forty-minute programmes. The first one is about native ponies. Second – the horse at work – heavy horses, farm horses, cab horses, war horses. The last is about the horse as our plaything. That's where the trekking sequences come in. Racing, show jumping, show horses and the Pony Club.'

'Something like the one that was on the BBC?' Petra asked brightly.

'Absolutely nothing like anything that has ever been done before,' roared Royce in mock fury. 'It is about the spirit of the horse. How it has changed our awareness of ourselves. Before there were cars the horse was the only form of transport. Can you imagine what it meant then to own a horse, any kind of horse? And a fast horse gave you wings. Set you above your mates. Changed your dreams. Gave you power and courage. That's what my film is about.'

Jinny listened entranced to Royce's enthusiasm. She couldn't imagine herself talking like that in front of Petra and Miss Tuke. She knew only too well how her thoughts could leap like wildfire in her mind, but she only told Shantih about them.

'By the last part the horse has become a toy. We've forgotten what it really is. I close the last film with shots of a gymkhana – kids screaming, plastic mums belching forth, ponies being pulled about, and then the awful noise of the Great Horses from Shaffer's play *Equus*, waiting to come back into their own.'

'Oh,' said Petra politely.

'I open the first film with a sequence on the horses painted in the caves of the Stone Age, and the Celtic cult of the Horse goddess Epona.'

'Like Jinny's horse statue!' exclaimed Sue. 'Wasn't that another of the Horse gods they worshipped?'

'What horse statue?' demanded Petra.

Petra knew nothing about the little metal statue of the Celtic Horse god that Jinny had found buried on the moors and had given to the Wilton Collection. The Wilton was only a small museum owned by an old man – Jo Wilton – who called his museum a sanctuary. The statue Jinny had found was in a glass case next to a small statue of Epona – a woman sitting sideways on a thickset pony, holding a fruit in her open hand. It was smooth and featureless, without detail. Quite often Jinny went back to the Wilton to stand in front of the two statues, thinking how strange it was that she should have been the one to find the Horse god when it had lain buried for thousands of years.

'It's a statue in the Wilton museum,' muttered Jinny, scowling at Sue, warning her to say no more; reminding her that she had sworn never to tell anyone about it. 'Next to Epona.'

'Sounds interesting,' said Royce. 'Let's hear about it, Jinny.'

A clock chimed in the hall. Royce shot out his

arm, glanced at a wafer of gold watch and sprang to his feet.

'Sorry. Have to go. Should be at Calmun by now. See you all Tuesday evening. Take care. Bye.'

'Typical,' said Miss Tuke. 'You've hardly told us a thing about what you want the ponies to do.'

Royce paused in his dash to the door.

'Smuggling sequence over the moor; stampede; standing at the door of a croft. That's about it. Oh, and the trekking shots. No hassle. You'll all be brill.'

Shouting goodbye, he was out of the house, and seconds later the roar of his sports car had faded away.

'Has not changed a bit,' stated Miss Tuke. 'Not in the least surprised that he's ended up like this. Only hope the film company is solvent.'

It was almost ten when they all came in from saying good night to the ponies. Jinny, walking beside Petra, and knowing that she should not say it, heard herself say, 'Fancy Royce knowing "The Arab's Farewell to His Steed" like that. Just fancy him knowing it when it is one of my most favourite poems.'

'You don't think he really liked that rubbish, do you?' said Petra. 'He was taking the micky. You didn't really think he was serious about it, did you?'

And Jinny knew that, as usual, she had fallen into the trap of saying things to Petra that she should have kept to herself.

Encouraged by Miss Tuke, Mrs Brothwick and Brian went straight to their rooms.

'Now let's get you three bedded down,' said Miss Tuke. 'One room with twin beds and one attic room. Who goes where?'

Petra, Sue and Jinny looked at each other. When Sue had stayed with the Manders at Easter there would have been no decision to be made. Sue and Jinny would have shared. Now there was an uneasy moment of silence.

'Sue is going to show me how to make up my eyes,' said Petra. 'So perhaps . . .?'

'That's OK, then,' said Jinny. 'I'd rather sleep in the attic,' and she followed Miss Tuke upstairs to a tiny room under the eaves.

Sitting on the edge of the bed Jinny could hear Sue and Petra giggling below her.

'Painting their eyes,' thought Jinny scornfully, to cover up the hurt emptiness inside her, for Sue was her friend, not Petra's. Petra shouldn't even be at Miss Tuke's. She had no right to come, pushing her way in and spoiling Jinny's holiday.

Even when she was in bed Jinny didn't feel like sleeping. She sat up, looking round the room. On the bedside table was a book of horror stories. Whenever Jinny had seen it she had turned it over so that she didn't need to look at the picture on the front. Now, almost against her will, she stretched across and turned the book over. The drawing on the cover was of a black horse rearing above a midnight house, a deserted house that stood alone on a bleak headland.

Jinny stared, fascinated. She picked up the book and opened it to see if there really was a story about a black horse in it. She shuddered, feeling the hairs rise on the back of her neck as she peered at the list of titles, almost too afraid to read them. The fourth story was called 'The Return of the Water Horse'. Jinny shivered convulsively, slammed the book shut, banged it back on the table, switched out the bedside lamp and pulled the bedclothes over her head.

She thought of Royce. She was sure Petra was

35

wrong. Royce had been enjoying the poem every bit as much as herself. Jinny wondered if he knew the one about the ghostly Border raiders who brought a riderless horse to the poet's house and challenged him to ride with them.

Sue's and Petra's voices gradually stopped. The house was silent but still Jinny could not sleep. It seemed as if she had lain for hours, tossing and turning, before she sat up again and switched on her light. The drawing on the book seemed to glow in the spotlight of the lamp. In the stables a pony whinnied, and in Jinny's imagination it was the Water Horse who stalked there – a creature, half man, half beast, bound by an evil mystery to haunt the night, luring its victims to their death in its underwater lair.

'Don't read it,' Jinny warned herself. 'Don't. You'll remember it when you're out alone at night.'

She picked up the book, opened it at 'The Return of the Water Horse' and began to read. She read how the daughter of the mansion house was left alone in the house, servants and parents being called away. The attic bedroom surrounded by Miss Tuke's common-sense security became the empty rooms of the mansion house. Creatures watched Jinny from the shadows. Beings without names were close, close behind her. Spirits, unseen by day, took visible form and waited inside the bedroom cupboard.

Jinny's gaze was glued by terror to the printed page. She heard the creak of the rusty hinges as the girl struggled in vain to close the storm doors. Jinny went back to the drawing room with the girl and sat in the oil lamp's glow, waiting, waiting. Far away on the moors the black horse rose from its underwater lair. Green slime-weed clotting its mane and tail, luminous eyes piercing the night, it galloped over the wind-swept moors. The girl, carrying her circle of lamplight, went from room to room, checking the bolted windows. The Water Horse, poised in the outer dark, watched the flickering light make its way throughout the house.

Jinny read on, transfixed with terror. She was the girl locked into the empty house. She felt the oil lamp in her hand, heard the creak of stairs under her feet.

The Water Horse came down from the moors. It galloped up the long drive. It struck at the door with a fore hoof, waited gaunt and ruined. The girl opened the door to a man in black clothing, weed entangled in his dripping, black hair. He gazed at her through luminous eyes.

'I am the Water Horse,' he said.

In the stables something disturbed one of the Highlands. It kicked out with an iron-shod hoof against the wood of its stall. Jinny heard the hoof strike her bedroom door; heard the creature cry, 'I am the Water Horse.' With all her strength she flung the book at the door and screamed for help.

Petra jumped out of bed, raced up the stairs and burst into Jinny's room.

'What on earth's the matter?' she demanded. 'What's wrong?'

The shaking body under the bedclothes did not reply. Petra saw the book and picked it up.

'Oh honestly, Jinny, don't tell me you've been reading horror stories again! You know you shouldn't. You know the way they upset you.'

Jinny risked a quick look over the bedclothes. Petra certainly looked like Petra, although it was always possible that she might be the Water Horse in her sister's shape.

'Come on, sit up. Get all that nonsense out of your head,' bossed Petra, and sitting up reluctantly, Jinny was sure that it was her sister.

'Leave your light on,' said Petra. 'I'm taking the book away so you won't start reading it again. Now get to sleep.'

Jinny nodded. The attic room was itself again.

'Say your tables through and dream of Royce,' said Petra, leaving Jinny's door open as she left.

'Cheek,' said Jinny, thinking that she disliked her sister more when she needed her than at any other time.

But when Petra had gone and Jinny was lying half asleep her mind strayed back to Royce. She would say, 'Do you know that poem about the Borderers, the one that begins . . .'

Trying to remember the exact words, Jinny fell asleep.

CHAPTER FOUR

Miss Tuke banged on bedroom doors at seven o'clock.

'Breakfast at eight. See to your ponies first.'

By the time Jinny reached the stables, Miss Tuke and Sue had already mucked out the Highlands who had been in all night.

'Tie the lot from the paddock to those rails,' Miss Tuke told Jinny. 'Knots in their halters. We'll give them all a feed.'

'Shantih isn't very keen on being tied up,' Jinny said. 'I'd be better to leave her in the field until we're ready to go.'

'Knew it,' declared Miss Tuke. 'She'll be nothing but trouble. Should never have let you bring her. Saved me leading two if you'd ridden Bramble and led Juno.'

Discreetly, Jinny said nothing. There would have been no point in coming if she had had to leave Shantih behind.

'Get the others tied up,' ordered Miss Tuke, and Jinny, clutching up halters, hurried to obey.

They ate breakfast as if they were swallows twittering on the brink of migration. Mrs Brothwick and Petra ate next to nothing, being more aware of nerves than hunger. Brian stoked up as if he were expecting a famine trek. Sue was herself again, chatting about the ponies, her new-found sophistication forgotten in the thrill of the start. Miss Tuke brisked about, her egg and bacon crammed into a morning roll, while she made a last-minute phone call to the farmer who was keeping his eye on the ponies that were being left behind, and pestered Mrs Scott with housekeeping details.

Mrs Scott looked after the house and made the meals for Miss Tuke's trekkers. From her calm seventy years Miss Tuke was a young thing, given to fussing about nothing.

'I will be here when you get back,' she assured Miss Tuke. 'It is not this week that I'm planning to make off with the silver.'

'Six trekkers arriving next Saturday. Up to you to settle them in, Scotty. We'll be back Saturday afternoon.'

'It will not be the first time I have seen to the trekkers,' Mrs Scott said.

Jinny thought how, by next Saturday, the trek would be over, filming with Royce would be in the past, not the future as it was now. They would all be back where they were.

'Dreaming again, Jinny! Snap out of it,' roused Miss Tuke.

The half-conscious thought drifted through Jinny's mind, that she had left the story of the Water Horse at its beginning. She would never know the end, for Petra had hidden the book. For all Jinny knew, the Water Horse might have brought good news to the girl.

'Jinny!' boomed Miss Tuke, dispersing the cobwebs of Jinny's dreams. 'I have one more phone call to make. So everyone down to the yard and start tacking up. Keep their halters on. Jinny and Sue will help.'

They took the ponies' tack from the rows of neatly labelled saddles and bridles in Miss Tuke's tack

40

room, and soon the yard was alive with noise. The ponies, sensing that this was no ordinary trekking day, played up. They stuck their heads in the air refusing to be bridled, blew themselves up so that their girths wouldn't meet. Fergus escaped from his stall with Mrs Brothwick in close pursuit, his bridle dangling from her arm. Beech, shifting in his stall, sent his ungirthed saddle crashing to the ground. Petra's high-pitched voice raged at him.

Miss Tuke descended on the chaos like an Assyrian tornado and order was restored. In ten minutes the ponies were tacked up, all the trekkers were wearing their haversacks containing packed lunches and the minimum of belongings each thought they would need for the trek.

'As usual,' sighed Miss Tuke as Jinny saddled Shantih.

'I was helping the others to get ready,' Jinny defended herself, but more to Shantih than Miss Tuke. She didn't want anyone mentioning the fact that she hadn't done much helping. She had been standing with her sketch pad and pencil, doing her best to catch the stir and tension of the yard. They were only rough sketches, but Jinny knew that when she wanted to make proper pictures of their trek they would be enough to bring every detail of the scene back into her mind's eye. She would be able to see it again as clearly as if she were standing watching it.

In Jinny's life there was Shantih; Finmory and her family; and then her drawing and painting. Jinny knew that she would go on making pictures all her life, that she was an artist, although she would have died rather than have said such a conceited thing aloud. When she was making a drawing that was right, it was like jumping Shantih, yet at the same time like sitting at home by the fire on a winter evening. When a painting leapt into life beneath her brush, she watched its creation from a still centre within herself, hardly knowing how she painted it.

'At last,' said Petra.

With a final chug at Shantih's girth, Jinny led her out of the paddock into the yard where the Arab flaunted brilliant as a bird of paradise surrounded by sparrows. Her tail was kinked over her back. The dry, mineral quality of her being was contained in damask silk and lustrous eye. Beside Shantih the trekking ponies were created from peat bogland and long days of mist and rain. Shantih sprang from the sun, fired by the desert's intensity.

'Now I'm telling you,' warned Miss Tuke. 'Any trouble from that idiot and you go straight back to Finmory. Brian can lead Bramble. You hear me?'

'Yes,' said Jinny, but couldn't. She could hear nothing for the thrill of the moment. It was about to begin.

Miss Tuke saw Petra, Mrs Brothwick and Brian safely mounted.

'I did hope I'd be on something with a bit more life in it than this pudding,' grumbled Brian, who had thumped down on McSporran's back like a sack of potatoes. 'I have done a lot of riding. Galloping and all that.'

'You told me,' said Miss Tuke. 'That's why I gave you McSporran. It takes a real rider to keep McSporran up with the others.'

'That's not what I meant . . .' Brian began, but Miss Tuke had left him and was holding Heather while Sue mounted Pippen.

Jinny had already untied Bramble from the rails. Holding his long halter rope she sprang on to

42

Shantih, controlled with seat and hands the moment when Shantih would have sprung into a trot, gathered her together and brought Bramble round to lead at her left side.

Miss Tuke brought her three ponies from their boxes. With the grey Misty on her left side, Juno's rope over Guizer's withers, Miss Tuke hauled herself on to Guizer's table-top back. Guizer clinked his bit, shaking his head at Juno, but stood stock-still until Miss Tuke had established herself securely in the saddle.

'Ready?' she challenged, casting her experienced eye over riders and ponies. 'Trek forward!'

Jinny rode behind Miss Tuke, her view nothing but bottoms. Mrs Brothwick worried aloud in case she had left her glasses behind, but no one was listening. Petra rode beside her, sitting stiffly upright, hands and heels correctly down. The hard hat she had borrowed from Miss Tuke sat at an angle on her brown curls, transformed into chic, fashionable headgear. Sue was behind Petra having trouble with Heather, who dragged at her rope's length, fearing Beech's heels. At the back of the trek McSporran moved like a thunder cloud – sullen and deliberate. The boy thumping about on his back was no concern of his. At a respectful distance, Mrs Scott shut the yard gate behind them.

They turned right when they reached the end of the track over Miss Tuke's land, out on to a narrow, metalled road, between high stone walls. Miss Tuke twisted round in her saddle.

'This is where we start praying,' she yelled back. 'Nothing but the Lord can help us if we meet traffic on this bit of road. Going to trot on until we reach the forestry. Steady trot. OK?'

Jinny felt Shantih drop behind the bit ready to rear. She sat down hard, trying to drive her forward as the irregular shuffle of walking hooves changed to a double beat. Bramble was already trotting, pulling at his halter rope.

'Get on with you,' Jinny cursed through clenched teeth, forcing herself not to use her heels, for she knew that if she did, Shantih would rear, stand straight up on her hind legs. Jinny heard the score of Shantih's shoes on the road as she overbalanced and crashed down; the panic as Shantih's forelegs caught in Bramble's halter rope; experienced the disgrace of being sent home when the trek had hardly started.

'Jinny, get on,' bossed Petra nervously. 'We've to trot. Didn't you hear Miss Tuke? *We* can't trot if you don't.'

Beech and Fergus crashed into Shantih, and the Arab plunged forward charging into Guizer.

'Warned you,' roared Miss Tuke, as Guizer lashed out, narrowly missing Jinny's knee. Shantih propped, searching for space to swing round, but the crush of trotting ponies closed her in. There was nowhere she could go, except forward. She arched her neck, tucked in her head, as Jinny, fingering her reins, brought her under control again. Light-hoofed amid the earth-pounding mass, Shantih trotted on.

'You know, she does nothing *but* ride Shantih and just look at her. You'd think she couldn't even trot,' Petra said to Mrs Brothwick.

'Failed your music exam,' thought Jinny, but said nothing.

'For this and all Thy mercies let us be truly thankful,' intoned Miss Tuke as they reached the gate to the forestry track without meeting any traffic. 'Brian, you are responsible for shutting gates.'

The ponies' hooves stirred the leaf mould into smells of autumn, lingering mustily in the riders' nostrils – smells of decay and fungus. The broad track ran between serried ranks of densely planted spruce trees.

'Not great trees but battery trees,' Jinny thought, remembering the gnarled pine trees that grew here and there about the moors. Suddenly, it was as if Jinny could see a group of three pine trees, their branches tortured by the wind into petrified arabesques. She could see the moor beyond the trees, textured with bracken, reaching out to the bulwark of the mountains. There was a dark figure walking swiftly through the bracken – a tall, angular man with a mane of glossy black hair and a gaunt, sunken face. Then, as if he knew Jinny was watching him, he turned and looked straight at her through green, light-filled eyes.

As swiftly as the vision had come, it went, leaving Jinny shivering in the sun.

'Never again,' she promised herself. 'I'm never, ever going to read another horror story as long as I live.'

At last they broke out from the confines of the forestry into the freedom of the moorland. Blue sky was high above them, sky laced with white clouds fanned out by the tide of the wind.

'Gallop!' demanded Shantih, crescenting the short moorland grass with urgent hooves.

'Not a chance,' Jinny told her. 'You've miles to go yet.'

Unconvinced, Shantih fretted and fussed, bumping into Guizer until Miss Tuke told Jinny to take her on in front and see if that would quieten her. At the head of the trek Shantih settled into a steady walk. Head held high she gazed about her, catching the least breath of movement – the tilt of a kestrel's wing as it waited on, high and almost motionless; hoodie crows that rose at their passing then dropped back on to grey boulders vivid with lichen; and the mountain sheep, lifting mild heads, lower jaws circling as they watched the intruders.

Jinny rode, a mounted chieftain leading her clansmen. Behind her, Brian demanded that they should gallop; Petra and Mrs Brothwick mentioned insistently that it was time for lunch.

They ate their packed lunches sitting on the hillside holding their ponies. Mrs Brothwick complained that she had pulled a muscle in her leg, and Petra told them all that her cleg-bitten ankles were beginning to swell. Brian told Sue, in a voice aimed at Miss Tuke, that if this had been the trail riding centre where he had spent his Easter holidays, they would all have galloped.

Miss Tuke beamed upon them. She told them that so far they had all put up a pretty good show, and chased them back on to their ponies as soon as she possibly could.

It was after six before they reached the road that led to Lillybank Guest House. The last mile had seemed endless. The hills which they had ridden over all day were shrouded in mist, the sky grey and louring, and even when Lillybank came into sight, its stone walls and towers seemed desolate and unwelcoming.

'Does it,' asked Mrs Brothwick suspiciously, 'have hot and cold running water?'

'All mod cons,' Miss Tuke assured her. 'Royce fixed it up for me.'

The drive to Lillybank wound between half-dead

oak trees, their trunks encrusted with mould. Hydrangeas and fuchsia grew in dank profusion. From behind the house they could hear the rush of a river. They rode up to the front of Lillybank and, through grimy windows, Jinny saw tables covered with starched tablecloths, laid with heavy, Victorian cutlery, and in the centre of each table a stained silver container filled with dusty, plastic flowers.

The front door opened and a maid in a grey dress and white apron told them to take their horses round the back where Miss Byng would see them.

'Not in the least what I was expecting,' Mrs Brothwick stated.

'Bet there's rats,' said Jinny, hoping that Petra would hear. But Petra was too worried about her swollen ankles to be bothered with any of Jinny's imaginings.

'Looks a bit of a dump to me,' said Brian. 'Are you sure they're expecting us?'

'Certain,' snapped Miss Tuke. She had dismounted and was having trouble towing her ponies up the path at the side of the guest house, the three Highlands being intent on pruning the overgrown shrubs.

'Have we to dismount?' Mrs Brothwick twittered. 'You know, I really do not think I can. I'm so stiff.'

Sue said in that case better to stay where she was, and Petra told them about the state of her ankles.

'Do keep up,' Miss Tuke shouted. 'Try to look like an organised trek not a disaster of refugees. Must say, I don't think much of Royce's idea of a guest house.'

The back of Lillybank was even more depressing than the front. It looked as if no sunlight ever reached it. Piles of junk – empty bottles, crates, plastic sacks – had settled down for life in decaying contentment. Rhododendrons and crumbling outhouses surrounded a back yard of slimy, green flagstones.

'What a pong!' exclaimed Petra.

'Told you there would be rats,' said Jinny.

'Brisk up,' rallied Miss Tuke. 'Remember some of us are here for free.'

'And some are not,' said Brian.

A tall gentlewoman with white hair, wearing tweeds and green wellingtons, opened the back door, told them they were an hour late and if they didn't hurry up they would be too late for dinner. Striding ahead, she pushed her way through the rhododendrons and led them to the field where the ponies were to spend the night. To Jinny's relief it was securely fenced with rusty, metal railings. She had imagined fencing as tumbledown as the guest house; had been ready to spend the night holding Shantih.

'Be in the dining room in half an hour,' Miss Byng warned them, after showing Miss Tuke the sack of oats and nuts that Royce had left in the corner of a shed. 'Any later and dinner will be over.'

'Saddles and bridles off,' Miss Tuke ordered. 'Check them over. Make sure they all have a drink at the burn over there, then bring them back here for a feed.'

Half an hour later, tack and boots dumped around the guest house stairs, hands hurriedly washed in the cloakroom, they were all sitting in the dark dining room which Jinny had seen from Shantih's back. There was no menu. The grey maid told them that they would have to make do with what was left.

After soup, so salty that Jinny could hardly

swallow it, soggy chips, cold roast meat swimming in tepid gravy, followed by blancmange and stewed rhubarb, the grey maid showed them to their rooms. Sue, Jinny and Petra were sharing.

'That was ghastly,' declared Petra. 'I would never have come if I'd known it was going to be like this.'

'No one asked you to,' muttered Jinny.

'It'll be much better in the hotel,' comforted Sue. 'This is only for one night.'

'But I must have a bath. I'm so stiff I can hardly move and my ankles are like balloons.'

Jinny looked without pity at Petra's cleg-bitten ankles. It served her right, pushing her way into Jinny's life. Riding was Jinny's thing. 'Bet she wouldn't have cared about me if I'd insisted on playing her piano all day and then moaned about my blistered fingers.'

Sue and Petra were lying flat out on top of their beds. Jinny was kneeling on her bed by the window. She pressed her face against the glass. The only good thing about their damp-smelling room was the view from the window. You could see over the ramparts of rhododendrons to the field where the ponies were grazing.

'We went to this night club when we were in Greece,' began Sue.

'I'm going down to see Shantih,' Jinny announced, and feeling in her anorak pocket to make sure she had her sketch pad and pencil, she marched across the room, banging the bedroom door behind her.

Outside Lillybank, Jinny stopped to draw its bleak walls and ivy-shrouded windows, all about to drown in the sea of advancing vegetation. A few cars were parked at the side of the drive so Jinny supposed that there must be other guests as well as themselves.

'Bet no one comes back twice,' she thought and remembered a short story she had read where a butcher hotel keeper killed off all his guests. That had been another horror story that Jinny shouldn't have read.

'If I were here alone,' she thought, 'I wouldn't stay. I'd get into my car and drive off. Wouldn't even let them know I was leaving, just in case.'

She found her way round to the back of the guest house, peered into one of the outhouses and saw a row of long-disused stalls. Miss Tuke had said that Lillybank used to be a shooting lodge, and Jinny supposed that the stabling would have been for the deer ponies. Jinny drew the row of stalls with their metal hayracks and stone troughs. Then she lightly touched-in the ghosts of the ponies who had once stood there. Long-dead eyes watched from the past; ears pricked to the sound of a kilted gamekeeper's footsteps; a hind foot clipped on wood.

In Jinny's imagination the Water Horse stood at the mansion-house door, waiting. In a grasp of blind panic Jinny spun round, dashed away from the stable, ran through the gripping fingers of the rhododendrons, vaulted over the iron railings; did not stop until she was standing with her arm over Shantih's withers.

'I am quite mad,' Jinny told her horse. 'Quite mad.'

Shantih blew warm breath over Jinny's hair, rubbing her head against Jinny's shoulder.

'Expect it's the same for you. Don't suppose Bramble understands the things you're afraid of. Expect you see things that Bramble never notices.'

Jinny lingered on, not wanting to go back to Sue and Petra and feel the odd one out. Tomorrow night she would see Royce again.

Jinny sketched Guizer shaking himself, Pippen dozing, McSporran delicately scratching his ear with a hind hoof.

'This is where the deer ponies must have grazed,' Jinny thought, and blinking her mind she brought the ghost ponies from their stalls to roll in the lush grass, shake tousled manes, stamp unshod hooves; their sides scarred by stag's antlers and galled by the bleeding burdens they had carried down from the hills.

The greying evening began to close in as Jinny made her way back to the guest house. Lillybank's lighted windows deepened the darkness. Suddenly she longed to be inside, safe with Petra and Sue. Pushing her way through the rhododendrons Jinny kept her mind fixed firmly on tomorrow. She thought about filming with the ponies and Royce, and wondered if he might want to film Shantih.

Coming out into the back yard Jinny paused. Lights were on in bedroom windows. She could hear a television's garbled noise. Safe again, Jinny took a last look round.

A man was leaning on the stable wall watching her. Tall and angular, black clothes folded about his bones, he seemed to grow from the shadows of the wall. His face, caught in a beam of light from a window, was gaunt and empty – flat cheekbones, a ridged nose, withered lips and green eyes that shone with an inward light beneath the fall of his coarse, black hair.

The man moved towards Jinny. She saw his lips open, but before he could speak, louder than the man's voice, Jinny heard the words in her own head, 'I am the Water Horse.'

She fled through the back door of Lillybank,

51

running blindly across a kitchen, along passages that led at last to the front of the guest house. She tore upstairs, yanked open the bedroom door. Petra was lying on her bed, slices of wet bread over her cleg bites. Sue was reading. Startled by Jinny's sudden appearance they both stared up at her.

'What now?' demanded Petra.

'Nothing,' said Jinny. 'Nothing.'

'You look scared stiff,' said Sue.

'Well I'm not. Miss Tuke said there was going to be cocoa and biscuits. I didn't want to miss them, that's all. What would I be scared of?'

'Sorry I spoke,' said Sue.

'Ignore her,' advised Petra. 'It'll be that ghost story she was reading last night.'

For minutes Jinny stood with her back against the door, then she crossed over to her bed, cupped her hands between the windowpane and her face, and looked out into the gathering darkness. Shantih was just visible. She was standing by the field gate staring intently at a dim figure walking towards her.

It was the man Jinny had seen in the backyard. As she watched, he reached the gate and stretched out his gaunt, maned head towards Shantih. The Arab arched her neck, reached out to him. They stood breathing, nostrils to nostrils.

'Quick,' Jinny screamed. 'Come quickly.'

But by the time Petra and Sue had reached the window the man had gone.

CHAPTER FIVE

Going into Lillybank's kitchen to ask for more bread, Jinny saw a hip-bath sitting on top of the cooker. In the water, like watching frogs, swam a host of poached eggs.

'Most guests don't ask for more bread at breakfast time,' said Miss Byng, who was still wearing her green wellies and seemed to rule supreme over Lillybank. 'I trust you're not feeding it to those animals?'

'Most guests aren't riding to Calmun in this downpour,' said Jinny. 'And anyway, the ponies wouldn't look at it. They're used to sugar.'

'Is that so?' said Miss Byng, unwillingly refilling the plate which Jinny had given to her, while the Cyclops eggs stared unblinkingly upwards.

'You're not to feed it to the ponies,' Jinny told them, putting the plate down on the table. 'And I shouldn't think she'd be too pleased if she knew Petra had been using bread to poultice her cleg bites.'

'I suppose you told her?' asked Petra.

'Might do,' said Jinny.

'Reckon she'd charge you for it,' grumbled Miss Tuke.

Outside, the rain cascaded from the rhododendrons, gushed round the sides of Lillybank and flowed in a torrent down the drive. The other guests in the dining room stared out despondently as they lingered over third cups of coffee.

'And they're only going to be sitting in cars,' Jinny thought.

Not one of the guests resembled the man she had seen last night. Once she had recovered from her fright, she had decided that he must have been a guest or someone who worked at Lillybank. It had just been chance that he had resembled the man in her daydream.

'Right, then,' announced Miss Tuke, rousing up the whole room. 'Enough of this slothing. It's not so bad when you're out in it.'

'It's worse,' said Sue, who had already been out with Miss Tuke feeding the ponies.

'Everyone at the front door in twenty minutes.'

Jinny wrapped her sketch pad in a plastic bag and buried it in the middle of her haversack. She would have no time for sketching today. Being ridden in rain like this always made Shantih more explosive than usual, and she would be worse today, surrounded by a horde of Highlands. Reluctantly Jinny pulled on her oilskins which were so crushed they looked as if an elephant had slept on them.

'Moon walker,' Jinny told herself, doing a monster walk in front of the wardrobe mirror.

'What are you doing now?' Petra demanded, opening the bedroom door and catching Jinny with her arms above her head and one massive, oil-skinned leg raised in a weightless stride.

'I'm coming.'

'You are not. You're messing about up here while we all hang around waiting for you.'

Jinny grabbed up her haversack and followed her sister downstairs. Petra's oilskin, identical to Jinny's, had spent yesterday neatly folded over the pommel of Petra's saddle; the night, hanging in the wardrobe.

Now it looked as if Petra had just bought it. Jinny put her tongue out at her sister's back. Petra had even managed to buckle a leather belt round her waist, changing her oilskin into a Mary Quant fashion garment, while Jinny's bulged huge and creased about her.

'Complete nonsense,' Miss Tuke was declaring to Miss Byng. 'I understood the film company had paid for everything.'

'Bedtime cocoa is extra,' stated Miss Byng. The folded bill held in her hand was a drawn sword barring their escape. 'Six mugs of cocoa, four plates of biscuits – ten pounds.'

'Daylight robbery,' snorted Miss Tuke. 'The first thing I do when I get home is expose this place to the Tourist Board.'

'Ten pounds,' said Miss Byng, gazing impassively over Miss Tuke's head.

Like a frantic wallaby, Miss Tuke dived through her layers of waterproofing and produced a ten pound note.

'Scandalous!' she declared. 'Utter disgrace!'

Still muttering to herself Miss Tuke led her trekkers down to the field.

'Get them tacked up as quick as you like,' she shouted, opening the field gate and stomping into the mass of rain-darkened ponies. 'Here, give me your halters and I'll catch them for you.'

Skilfully Miss Tuke slipped halters round unwilling heads, knotted halter ropes, and with a hearty slap on spongy shoulder or rump, handed the Highlands on to their riders. She was left holding her own three ponies and Bramble as she watched Jinny desperately trying to catch Shantih.

'She can't bear the rain!' Jinny gasped as Shantih

flung herself away and star-fished down the field.

'Get the rope round her neck,' shouted Miss Tuke.

'What does she think I'm trying to do?' Jinny muttered. Already the rain had found its way down the neck of her oilskin, and her left jodh boot was filling with water. Although Shantih was never very keen on being ridden in a gale she was never difficult to catch. Something else seemed to be troubling her, something or somebody on the moors.

'Put your halter behind your back,' suggested Petra.

'Oh yes,' said Jinny, turning on her sister. 'You know all about it, don't you? You know all about horses, don't you? You bloomin' well know everything.'

'Come and help the others,' said Miss Tuke sharply. 'No point in chasing her round. Let her settle.'

Yet even when Jinny threw down the halter and went to help Mrs Brothwick, Shantih didn't calm down. Nostrils wide, eyes bursting from her head, she raked up and down the far side of the field, paying no attention to the trekking ponies. Every now and again she would stop and whinny wildly over the grey reaches of moorland, then stand listening tensely, and when there was no reply, go back to her ragged, battering trot.

'Up you get, as soon as you're ready,' called Miss Tuke, and Jinny hung, with all her weight, on to Mrs Brothwick's off-side stirrup, while Mrs Brothwick pulled herself into the saddle.

'I do hope you are going to be able to catch that horse of yours. You can see how she's upsetting Fergus,' said Mrs Brothwick, looking like a chess piece in her brand-new riding coat.

Fergus looked to Jinny as if he was about to go to sleep. He had manoeuvred himself with his quarters to the gale, and was standing with his head drooping, resting a hind foot. He looked as if the last trump wouldn't have bothered him too much.

'Try again, now,' called Miss Tuke. 'If you can't catch her, you'll have to ride Bramble and leave her here.'

'Never!' Jinny shouted back.

Leaving the halter lying on the grass, Jinny walked slowly towards Shantih. A little way from her Jinny stood still, held out her open hands to her horse and spoke loving nonsense to her in a slow voice. Shantih stood still and turned her head, listening to Jinny.

'Oh the horse, the horse. Steady then, steady. Quiet the woman. Come on with us now. Steady Shantih, steady.'

The rain raged down against Jinny but she stood still, conscious of the others watching her, of their barely controlled impatience.

'Come on then, the lass. Whoa Shantih.'

The slow murmur of Jinny's voice created an invisible link between herself and Shantih. It drew the horse towards her. Stepping slowly, reluctantly, Shantih walked up to Jinny.

'Fool horse,' said Jinny, scratching Shantih's withers. 'Of all the mornings you had to choose this one.'

Jinny scratched along Shantih's mane until her hand closed on the wisp of forelock and Shantih was caught.

Ignoring Brian's remarks on horse hypnotism and Petra apologising to everyone for all the delay her sister was causing, Jinny tacked Shantih up, mounted and took Bramble from Miss Tuke.

'By gracious permission of Miss Manders – trek forward!' cried Miss Tuke, turning her phalanx of Highlands and leading the way out of Lillybank. Jinny tucked Shantih in behind her. She sat firm and tight in the saddle, one hand heavy on the reins, the other hand controlling Bramble, keeping him neatly in beside her, making him pay attention.

They rode along a narrow road, protected from the worst of the weather by a stone wall and trees. Then, turning off the road, they followed a twisting path through the trees that took them out on to the moors where, hardly visible through the grey, sheeting rain, a track curved away in front of them.

Shantih whinnied longingly, gazing over the bleak expanse, the tips of her ears almost touching as she listened for any reply. Jinny sat down hard in the saddle, gathered her horse together between hands and seat.

'Oh no you don't,' she warned. 'There's nothing on the moors for you.'

Shantih danced impatient fore feet; tightened her cold back, threatening to buck.

'Not on your life,' Jinny told her.

She controlled Shantih's excitement as firmly as she turned her own mind away from thoughts of the man she had seen last night. He *must* have been someone who worked at the guest house, someone who liked horses. Last night when Sue and Petra had come to the window, Jinny had pretended that she had wanted them to see Shantih. She knew Petra would only laugh at her if she tried to tell her about the weird stranger; would say it was all Jinny's imagination, as her daydream of the same dark figure striding across the moors had been.

'Control yourself,' Jinny growled, both to Shantih and herself.

'Trot on,' Miss Tuke shouted. 'Brian, keep McSporran up.'

Miss Tuke, her three ponies well under her control, leant into the wind, urging Guizer on with tight kicks of her booted heels.

Jinny rode Shantih at a sitting trot. Her bare hands holding reins and halter rope ached under the icy rain. Her left foot slurped in its rain-filled boot. The collar of her oilskin chafed against her neck.

'And there's hours to go,' she thought. 'Hours of this before we reach Calmun.'

Jinny was used to riding in any sort of weather, but when she was alone she could gallop and jump, send the blood coursing through her body to lift her spirits and make her forget the wind and rain. Not this slow drag of walking and trotting; of fighting to keep Shantih behind Guizer, for today Miss Tuke hadn't suggested that Jinny should lead the trek.

Crouching down in her saddle, Jinny looked round at Petra who was sitting stiffly upright, and at Sue riding at her side, chatting, while Pippen trotted calmly into the rain.

'Bet they're talking about make-up,' Jinny thought bitterly.

Suddenly Brian came up from behind Petra. He was holding his reins in one hand, swinging the slack of his reins from side to side on McSporran's neck. In his other hand he carried a long bracken frond which he was flapping against McSporran's quarters.

Miss Tuke scowled round.

'Enough of that,' she shouted. 'Throw that away.'

'What?' demanded Brian, laughing as he dropped the bracken and kicked McSporran level with Shantih. 'I haven't got a thing. Just catching up like you told me to.'

'Don't know how I got stuck on this dud,' he said to Jinny. 'How about a swop? I'd fancy a ride on yours.'

'No chance,' said Jinny.

'I've done a lot of riding, you know. Been trail riding and all that. You'd enjoy trail riding. Mostly galloping. Hope the filming is going to be better than this. My autumn week, you know, and a bit of a waste up to now, must say.'

Although Brian was speaking to Jinny he obviously intended Miss Tuke to hear as well.

'It's not so much the ponies,' he almost shouted. 'It's being looked after by a bloomin' nurse maid all the time.'

'When you show signs of being responsible,' began Miss Tuke, turning on Brian, her eyes glaring from the porthole of her cagoule. 'Then I shall consider . . .'

At the moment when Miss Tuke's whole attention was beamed on to Brian, a grouse burst out of the bracken under Guizer's nose. In rattling, squawking terror it flung itself into the air. Four more grouse exploded in its wake. Guizer shied violently. Miss Tuke sailed over his head, reins and halter ropes torn from her grasp.

Jinny grabbed at flying ropes but missed them. For a second she was aware of nothing but the plunging, escaping ponies. Then she looked round, expecting Miss Tuke to be up on her feet organising their capture. Unbelievably, Miss Tuke was still lying face down in the heather.

Sue, Jinny, Petra and Mrs Brothwick crowded round her and there was a moment of absolute silence as they all sat staring down at her. It had happened so suddenly, as if during the blink of an eye a television set had switched channels, changing everything.

Sue and Petra flung themselves off their ponies.

'Don't touch her,' warned Mrs Brothwick, lowering herself stiffly to the ground and advancing on Miss Tuke, the shrouds of her riding coat creaking about her.

'She can't just lie there,' said Petra, crouching at Miss Tuke's side.

'It's in case she's broken anything,' said Mrs Brothwick.

'Took a right purler,' said Brian, not looking at Miss Tuke where she lay lumped on the ground.

Mrs Brothwick put her arm round Miss Tuke's shoulders, easing her from the ground, and Jinny saw blood pouring from a huge gash above Miss Tuke's right eye.

'We've got to get the bleeding stopped,' said Mrs Brothwick, loosening the hood of Miss Tuke's cagoule. 'Give me anything you have that I can pad it with. Anything.'

Mrs Brothwick pressed the towels Petra and Sue gave her against Miss Tuke's forehead, but, almost as they touched the wound, the dark swell of blood oozed through.

'It's no use,' said Jinny.

She was still sitting astride Shantih, staring in disbelief at the limp puppet-figure that a few minutes ago had been Miss Tuke.

'We'll need to get a doctor,' said Mrs Brothwick. 'Fast.'

'I'll go,' cried Jinny.

She threw Bramble's halter rope at Brian, swung Shantih round and rode at a full gallop, back towards the guest house. The wind was behind them, and the rain driving against Shantih's quarters sped her on.

'She could die,' Jinny thought. 'Could bleed to death.'

She drove Shantih on towards the path through the trees.

'Faster,' she urged. 'Faster.'

'So much blood,' she thought, screwing her mind against the picture of Miss Tuke's unnatural stillness and the blood pouring down her face. 'The rain makes it look worse,' Jinny told herself, but it wasn't rain that had seeped so quickly through Mrs Brothwick's makeshift padding.

Leaning close to Shantih's neck, Jinny galloped through the trees, reached the road and sent Shantih galloping on towards Lillybank. The tattoo of Shantih's hooves fired Jinny's urgency as they stormed up the drive to Lillybank.

Jinny threw herself from the saddle. Holding the buckle of Shantih's reins she raced up the steps, struggled to open the front door and screamed into the dim hallway.

'There's been an accident! Quick! Quick! We've got to get a doctor at once.'

A middle-aged couple came suspiciously down the stairs.

'It's Miss Tuke,' Jinny shouted. 'She's bleeding to death. We must get a doctor.'

'We're only . . .' began the man, as Miss Byng came through from the back of the guest house.

Jinny saw herself reflected in the hall mirror, her red hair plastered down her back, her eyes wild in her muddied face as she blurted out the story of Miss Tuke's accident.

Miss Byng's green wellingtons took her efficiently to the phone. She dialled crisply, without hesitation and stood tapping her fingernails against the brass ornaments that surrounded the phone. She regarded Jinny with the same look of remote distaste she had worn when Jinny had asked her for more bread.

'We have a car,' said the man on the stairs. 'Would it help?'

'Answer. Answer,' prayed Jinny. 'Let the doctor be there. Please. Please.'

'Ah, Doctor,' said Miss Byng, and Jinny felt her knees sink beneath her. Weak with relief she leant against the door, could hardly answer when Miss Byng handed her the phone and the doctor questioned her about the accident.

'I'll be at Lillybank's gates in a few minutes,' he said, and before Jinny could thank him he had put the receiver down.

Jinny waited at the gates, time stretched so taut she could hardly breathe. Every minute that Jinny waited, Miss Tuke was lying helplessly on the ground.

'He's taking so long. My fault if she bleeds to death. My fault for not getting here quicker. Oh hurry, hurry. Now. Come now.'

She kept Shantih walking up and down, ready to gallop ahead of the doctor the second he arrived.

A battered Range Rover came speeding into sight through the rain. It stopped violently by Shantih's side, making her shy and spook.

'Where's the casualty?' demanded a ginger-headed man with a spiky moustache.

'This way,' and Jinny let Shantih surge forward.

The Range Rover followed them along the path through the trees, and when Jinny pointed the way over the hillside it roared ahead of her into the sheeting rain.

Although Jinny reached Miss Tuke only minutes after the doctor, he had already padded Miss Tuke's wound with huge wads of cotton wool and was winding a bandage round her head. Miss Tuke was still unconscious.

'Got to get her into hospital at once. It's a deep kick and in a nasty place on her temple. Probably need some blood as well. One of you will have to come with me.'

'I'll come, Doctor,' volunteered Mrs Brothwick, abandoning Fergus as if he had been a parked car, her voice bright with relief. 'I have Red Cross experience.'

The doctor brought a stretcher from the Range Rover, unrolled it beside Miss Tuke, and Jinny watched her being lifted on to it and stowed into the Range Rover. Her arm dangled lifelessly and most of her face was lost beneath the monstrous bandaging.

'Will you kids manage on your own?' the doctor called, hardly waiting for an answer before he scorched away.

Watching the Range Rover disappear into the shrouding mist, Jinny could hardly believe it had happened, that Miss Tuke was lying unconscious, being taken to hospital.

'Now,' said Petra. 'We'd better get this lot sorted out. I only hope Lillybank will let us leave them in their field.'

'Leave them!' exclaimed Jinny in astonishment. 'What do you mean, leave them? We've got to get them all to Calmun. Royce and the film company are there now, expecting us to arrive tonight. We've to be filmed tomorrow.'

'Not now this has happened,' said Petra. 'Of course we can't manage eight ponies by ourselves.

We don't even know the way there.'

'The map's in Miss Tuke's saddlebag,' said Brian. 'I can find the way from a map. I've done a good bit of orienteering in my day.'

'Don't be so stupid,' snapped Petra. 'We can't possibly go on without Miss Tuke. Say we'd another accident? Out on the moors where we couldn't get help?'

'Say they drop the bomb?' said Jinny. 'We must go on. Miss Tuke needs the money. I'm not going back.'

'I tell you I can find the way all right,' insisted Brian.

Jinny looked straight at Sue. 'Well?' she said. 'What about it?'

'Be an adventure,' said Sue, grinning.

'That's it then,' crowed Jinny. 'Three against one. Trek forward.'

CHAPTER SIX

'It's no use arguing about it,' stated Sue. 'If we're wrong, we're wrong and there's nothing else for it except to go back.'

They had been riding for about an hour along the hill track that Brian had assured them would lead to the Pass of the Horses which was clearly marked on Miss Tuke's map.

'There's the track we're on and that's the one we should be on. It's obvious. We should be there with mountains on each side of us,' stated Petra.

From the beginning she had disagreed with Brian, and at last, convinced that they were riding the wrong way, she had insisted that they stop and have another look at the map.

The pouring rain of the early morning had changed to a steady drizzle, but Jinny was too wet for it to make much difference.

'You mean we've to go all that way back?' she moaned.

'We could have gone this way,' said Brian, hoping to take their attention away from his mistake. 'If we'd followed that track from the trekking centre we could easily have reached Calmun in one day. It isn't all that far if we'd gone that way.'

'It was meant to be a trek,' said Jinny. 'Not getting to Calmun by the quickest route. Another family was coming instead of us. That's why Miss Tuke chose this way. Only now there's only you. *We* shouldn't be here at all.'

And Jinny thought how different it would have been if they hadn't come on the trek. She would have been riding with Sue, jumping Shantih, letting Sue see how Shantih could almost, very nearly almost, do a perfect turn on the forehand. There would have been no Petra, spoiling it all; no Miss Tuke lying on the ground with a bleeding head; no dark stranger haunting the edges of her life.

'I was right all the time,' said Petra. 'I knew we shouldn't have come this way.'

'Then let's stop going on about it and get back on to the right track,' insisted Sue.

Jinny turned Shantih and set off the way they had just ridden. Her arms ached from urging Bramble on and holding Fergus back.

'Now they're all sure they're going home,' Jinny thought, as both her lead ponies started forward at a trot and Shantih plunged to follow them.

Brian, who had reorganised himself on to Guizer, was leading Misty and Juno. Sue riding Pippen led Heather, while Petra dragged McSporran along behind Beech.

'Don't think I wouldn't like to gallop,' Jinny assured Shantih. 'I'd like nothing better than a good gallop but that would mean loose ponies all over the moors. 'We wasted enough time catching Misty and Juno.'

Jinny hunched her shoulders, set her feet home in her stirrups and held Shantih to a spring-heeled walk.

By the time they reached the fork where they had gone wrong, the rain had stopped, and a watery sun shone through veils of mist. A breeze sprang up and they rode through dense patches of mist that vanished in a second to reveal vistas of rain-sparkling moorland.

'Anyone for lunch?' Brian asked.

'I've looked,' said Sue. 'It's poached egg in between stale bread.'

'Yuk,' said Jinny. 'Definitely no!'

'I don't think we should stop,' said Petra. 'We've still to get down the hillside to Calmun. Miss Tuke was worried about getting down even when we would have had plenty of time to spare. If we don't push on we'll be trying to get down in the dark.'

'It's marked on the map,' said Brian. 'Don't worry, I'll know where it is.'

A hollow silence greeted his words. 'Big deal,' thought Jinny as they rode on. 'Brian will know the way. Big deal.'

There was no doubt now, they were certainly on the right track and approaching the Pass of the Horses. On either side high hills rose up about them. The short, moorland grass clung around the edges of scree and boulders that rose up into barren rock, streaked with the white force of falling water. Sheep seen high above their heads were poised on outcrops of rock like mountain goats. The double note of a curlew echoed mournfully through the mist.

Shantih had settled. She walked steadily forward, her ears sharp, ignoring the ponies jog-trotting at her sides. Jinny was thinking about Royce. She imagined what it would be like to be as smooth and sophisticated as he was; to be making your own film, knowing enough to make actors and cameras turn your own private dream into a film that would be shared by millions. She imagined the film she would make about Shantih. She would ask Royce about it.

As they rode into the pass, silence closed about them. Petra, who had been chatting nervously to Brian about their descent to Calmun, stopped talking. Immediately behind Jinny, Sue changed from singing 'One man went to mow' to 'Oh never leave me', and then her voice trailed into silence.

Glimpsed through the wreathing mist the sides of the pass towered high above them, dwarfing the cavalcade of ponies and riders. The picture of Miss Tuke lying so still on the ground, blood oozing from her head, trickling down her face, came back clearly into Jinny's mind and would not go away. Royce, the filming and the longed-for warmth and luxury of food seemed no more than a mirage which they would never reach.

A stir of wind blew from behind them, momentarily blinding Jinny with her own hair, clearing the way ahead.

The man in the black clothes was walking ahead of them. Jinny felt her flesh clutch to her bones. He was only visible for a second and then the curtains of mist swept back again, hiding the figure from her sight.

'Did you see him?' Jinny cried, turning back to Sue. 'In front of us. A man walking in front of us?'

'What?'

'That man in black clothes.'

'You must be joking.'

'I saw him,' insisted Jinny. 'He's there just ahead of us.'

'You imagined you saw him,' said Sue. 'It must have been the mist made you think there was someone there. The way it's moving.'

Jinny said no more. She knew she had seen the man as clearly as she had seen him outside Lillybank last night.

'Perhaps he's a hiker,' Jinny told herself. 'A perfectly normal hiker, who just happens to be going the same way as ourselves. If I hadn't read that story about the Water Horse I wouldn't be thinking all this nonsense.'

But in spite of her commonsense advice, Jinny glanced nervously from side to side as they rode on through the pass. She searched the mist for any movement of the dark figure, but there were only sheep jangling Jinny's nerves as they ran, stiff-legged, away from the ponies, and once an eagle dropping from the mists to check up on the intruders in his mountain fastness.

Coming out of the pass they left the mists behind them. Moorland and rockfall shone brilliantly after the rain, and low sun stroked the landscape with light.

'You can see why Royce wanted to come here to film,' said Brian, dismounting and staring out over the dramatic scenery that spread before them. 'Takes your breath away, doesn't it?'

Jinny was too busy searching for any sign of the stranger to reply. Petra was staring fixedly down to where, far below them, a cluster of cottages and a white-walled hotel were just visible. Sue didn't even hear him. She was eating cold poached egg from a soggy, greaseproof bag, with total concentration.

Jinny realised how hungry she was. So hungry that even Lillybank's cold poached eggs would be better than nothing. She took the food out of her haversack and began to eat it.

'We haven't to ride down there, have we?' demanded Petra, and Jinny knew from her sister's voice that she was terrified.

'Give the ponies a breather,' said Brian, taking out the map and spreading it over Guizer's saddle. 'We'd better all look at it. I don't fancy having to turn round and come back from down there.'

Stretching back her head as far as it would go, Jinny could hardly see the top of the mountains that rose above them, while beneath her feet the hillside fell away like the slide at Hickstead.

'We're here?' said Brian, putting his finger on the map and looking up at Petra. 'Miss Tuke has marked it with a cross.'

'Those roofs you can see must be Calmun,' agreed Petra, hanging on to Beech's reins and McSporran's halter rope as she stretched across to see the map. 'But we can't possibly ride down there. It's far too steep.'

'They'd break their legs,' agreed Sue. 'Miss Tuke could never have meant us to go straight down there.'

'Straight is the only way.' said Jinny. 'Only dangerous if you let them wander about or get out of control.' She would have ridden Shantih down without thinking twice about it.

'We must get to Calmun somehow,' said Brian.

'But there's not even a path,' said Petra. 'Let's ride on a bit. There might be some kind of track.'

'Can't waste too much time,' said Brian. 'We don't want to have to ride down in the dark.'

'Really, it's not all that steep,' Jinny said. 'It just gets steeper the more you look at it. I'll go first.'

But Petra was already back on Beech, and lugging a reluctant McSporran behind her, was riding further along the track. The others followed.

'It's stupid,' Jinny thought, trying to organise a reluctant Bramble. 'We've got to get down somewhere. Better to push on with it instead of messing around like this.'

Petra led the way along the track. Even when Beech performed a spectacular curtsey that would normally have made her hang back and let someone else take the lead, she still pushed on. Jinny, catching a glimpse of her face as she looked round to urge on McSporran, saw the tightness of her lips and nostrils, her slanted eyebrows tensely wrinkled together, and knew that her sister was scared stiff.

'It's no use,' Sue shouted when they had been riding for about a quarter of an hour. 'We're going further away from Calmun all the time. Miss Tuke must have meant to ride down there.'

'Let's go on just a bit,' Petra pleaded.

'No!' said Jinny, 'we're wasting time. Better get down now before it starts getting dark.' And ignoring Petra's protests she turned Shantih, Bramble and Fergus and led the way back.

They stood, grouped together, staring towards Calmun.

'It's having ponies to lead,' said Sue. 'I could manage Pippen OK. It's having to lead Heather.'

'Rubbish!' snapped Jinny. 'They know each other well enough by now.'

She wanted to add that if they started being afraid they'd had it, for Petra's fear was like the mist, spreading everywhere, touching now one, now the other, making the most ordinary objects monstrous.

'We could lead them,' suggested Sue. 'If only Miss Tuke was here she'd know what to do.'

'Well she's not,' stated Jinny. 'And leading them would be the worst thing. We'd never manage to hold them. No saying where they'd end up.'

'What's bothering me,' muttered Brian, 'is having to lead two of them down.'

For a split second Jinny saw Fergus cross in front of Shantih, felt Shantih's legs catch in the halter rope before she pitched forward, and Jinny was caught in

72

a welter of falling ponies and threshing hooves as she went rolling down the hill to lie at the bottom as silent and still as Miss Tuke.

'Couldn't we go back?' said Petra, asking the impossible as if it were possible.

'We'd know the way,' said Sue. 'That's one thing.'

They stood looking guiltily at each other.

'We could trot most of the way,' said Brian. 'The ponies would know they were going home.'

Their nerves drew them closer together, made the hillside drop seem as if they stood poised on the peak of Everest.

Suddenly Jinny realised what they were about to do – to ride back through the Pass of the Horses, riding blindly in the dark, every stride haunted by the sinister presence of the dark stranger, when there, below them, was Calmun Hotel – lights and voices and Royce. Royce. Blond hair and laughing eyes. She would say, 'Do you know the poem about the Border Raiders . . .' And Royce would know it. They would recite it together.

'Honestly,' Jinny exclaimed. 'If Miss Tuke could see us. Don't be so daft. Of course we can ride down. S'easy. If they knew there was a feed waiting for them they'd have galloped down ages ago.'

'We can't . . .' began Petra.

'I'll go first,' said Jinny. 'Most important thing is to keep them walking and keep them going straight.'

'Jinny don't!' cried Petra.

'Fear not, little flock,' Jinny teased, mocking her sister. 'Follow me,' and gathering up Shantih's reins, a halter rope in each hand, Jinny turned Shantih off the track and began the descent.

The Arab stretched stiff forelegs, stepping cautiously, her head reaching and low.

'It's nothing,' praised Jinny. 'On you go, Horse. Horse of the Gods. Golden Horse. Shantih Sky Walker. Walk out. On you go.'

Jinny felt Shantih's delicate mouthing of the bit as she took tight, insecure steps. The land fell away below, roof steep. Bramble and Fergus kept pace beside Shantih, making nothing of the drop.

Jinny heard Sue, Pippen and Heather coming down behind her. She heard Petra scream to Beech to take care, and Brian give an idiotic cowboy whoop to cover up his fear.

'It's nothing,' Jinny yelled back to Sue, but as she shouted, Fergus shied, knocking into Shantih, making her stumble, her muzzle brushing the ground before she regained her balance. In that moment Jinny felt the pull of the space beneath her; how they stepped into air. Was suddenly afraid for Shantih, in case she should fall and injure herself.

'If only Miss Tuke were here,' Jinny thought desperately, but as far as Jinny knew Miss Tuke was lying in hospital. There was only herself, Jinny Manders, to lead the way down.

'Keep back,' Jinny called. 'Don't come too close.'

She concentrated on her riding. At first she had sat back as she had seen French cavalry officers doing, in photographs of them riding down a slide. Then, seeing how Bramble and Fergus splayed their hind legs, giving themselves a secure base, Jinny gradually sat forward, balancing herself over Shantih's withers, taking care not to interfere with her mouth in any way.

They were over halfway down when the hill became steeper. It seemed an almost vertical drop to the level ground beneath them. Fergus pulled at the length of his rope, fighting against Jinny. Then he

74

came plunging forward, knocking against Shantih to check his speed. Bramble sprang away.

'Get on with you,' Jinny muttered through clenched teeth. She had almost lost control of the ponies. Her knees, after the long day's riding, were loose against the saddle. Her feet jammed in the stirrups swung weakly outward. She pressed her knuckles hard against Shantih's neck, seeing nothing but Shantih's fringe of mane and pinned-back ears; hearing her anxious, snorting whinny as Shantih crept forward. Jinny could only sit helplessly in the saddle, refusing to give way to the fear that threatened to engulf her.

'I can't hold him,' Petra screamed, her voice high and surprising as a bird at night-time. 'Can't . . .' and Petra's words were lost in a batter of hooves.

Trailing his halter rope McSporran came tanking down behind Jinny, jolting and tossing his head wildly as he drew level with her.

'Whoa!' Jinny shouted. 'Whoa!' but her voice was drowned by Petra's screams. Beech, totally out of control, skidded and sprawled behind McSporran. Petra, her face as white as paper, was clinging to his neck.

'I can't hold Shantih,' Jinny thought desperately. 'If they get in front of me I can't stop her.'

Sue and Brian came charging after Petra, Guizer snaking his head, twisting his quarters. Glancing back Jinny saw the buck that tossed Brian over Guizer's head. She saw Guizer stumble and fall. A madness of loose ponies surged around Jinny as she felt Shantih start to plunge.

The call came from the direction of the road. It was a man's voice and yet a voice without words. First a high, imperious call, then a low, gentle sound.

At the first cry the ponies stood still. Shantih froze, only an answering whinny trembled her nostrils. Brian jumped to his feet, Petra pushed herself back into the saddle. Then, as the second call reached them, all the ponies, Shantih and Pippen, began to move. As slowly as dream horses breasting through liquid air, they walked down the hillside until they reached the land that bordered the road.

Round the corner of the road came Royce's scarlet sports car. It spun to a halt with a skid of tyres. Royce, a blonde girl and two young men burst out of it.

'Am I pleased to see you!' exclaimed Royce. 'We've been expecting you for hours. We heard from Mrs Brothwick about Auntie Tuke's accident and then no sign of you lot.'

'You didn't ride down there?' asked the girl, taking in Petra's parchment face, Brian's mud-smeared clothes, and the loose ponies dragging their halter ropes.

'Did you call us?' demanded Jinny. 'Shout before you came round the corner?'

Royce shook his head. 'No,' he said, taken aback by Jinny's urgency. 'Why?'

'We were in a bit of a mess,' Brian answered. 'Things were getting rather out of hand. Then the ponies heard something and suddenly they all calmed down. Guess it must have been the car they heard. Realised they were almost on the road.'

'Thank goodness they did,' gasped Petra. 'I couldn't have stayed on any longer,' and she laughed – high, nervous laughter.

'We could all have been injured, killed,' Jinny thought, seeing in her mind's eye ponies with broken legs, damaged backs. Petra falling, Brian trampled, herself lying on the ground, the blind, iron-shod feet of the ponies flashing about her face. Only a split second more and the disaster would have happened.

'Hearing a car wouldn't have calmed them down like that,' said Sue, who was the only one who had managed to stay in control. 'Even Pippen was beginning to get worked up.'

'Might have been another horse,' suggested Brian.

'More likely to make them more excited,' said Sue.

'They're discussing it as if it was an ordinary happening,' Jinny thought. 'As if there could be some reasonable explanation for it,' and she searched the lower reaches of the hillside for the least movement that might have been the dark stranger. For a second she was sure that she saw him and then he had disappeared.

'It must have been him,' Jinny thought, seeing his bleak face, heavy mane of hair, the gnarled hand that had stretched out to grip her when she had fled into Lillybank; the weirdness there had been about him. 'He would have had the power to stop them.'

'How is Miss Tuke?' Petra asked, and Royce said that he had phoned the hospital to be told she had been stitched up, recovered consciousness and was being X-rayed. He was to phone back later for more information.

Royce drove the car back to the hotel. The blonde girl, whom Royce had introduced as Sally, his Production Assistant, and the other two – Alec the cameraman and Don the assistant cameraman – walked back to the hotel with them. Jinny, walking at Shantih's head, thought that the day had been going on forever. Breakfast at Lillybank seemed to belong to the distant past but was only that morning.

Sally and the two men stayed to help them water and feed their ponies; showed them where to leave their tack and took them down to the field where they were to be turned out.

'There were trekking ponies in it last summer,' Sally assured them. 'And I've checked out the fences myself.'

'Should think they feel like me,' said Petra. 'Ready to collapse.'

'How about baths first?' Sally asked as they walked towards the hotel. 'Dinner is at our expense so choose what you like. You deserve it after the day you've had. Then join us in the lounge. I know Royce wants to discuss tomorrow's filming with you.'

Holding her after-dinner coffee cup in her hand, Jinny stood uncertainly behind Sue, Petra and Brian. The others had abandoned their coffee but Jinny had hung on to hers and now felt that she shouldn't have. Really she wanted to take it up to bed with her, finish it in bed and then sleep. The only spare clothes Jinny had brought with her were a pair of jeans. Not too clean before she'd stuffed them into her haversack and now crushed and damp, they looked outstandingly disgusting beside Petra's smart little dress.

'At least they didn't have time to paint their eyes,' Jinny thought, as Royce waved to them from a table close to the glass patio doors at the far end of the hotel lounge.

'Sit down, sit down,' he greeted them. 'I've been on the phone to Mrs Scott and spoken to Mrs Brothwick who is staying at the trekking centre for the rest of the week. Latest communication from Auntié Tuke is that her X-rays are clear and she intends to return home tomorrow. Age is catching up with the old bird. A year or two ago, she would have been out tonight.'

Royce ordered a Coke for Sue, a shandy for Petra, lager for Brian and another round of drinks for himself and Sally.

'No thanks,' Jinny said when he asked her. 'I'll finish my coffee.'

She knew it was the wrong thing to say but she didn't care. Now she was actually sitting with Royce, his blue eyes and wing of fair hair that she had been dreaming about were suddenly too real, too close. She drew back into her own centre, peered out critically at Brian chatting to Petra, Sally laughing, talking in too loud a voice so that other hotel guests noticed her and turned to smile.

'Isn't this what you wanted, being with the people that other people admire?' Jinny asked herself. 'Isn't this the glamour of filming?'

At another table nearby, film extras, pointed out to them by Sally, watched Royce from the corner of their eyes. The girls at the table talked as brightly as Sally, aware of Royce's presence. It was all false, tied on with tinsel. Ken would have despised it.

Jinny turned away. She stared at their reflections in the glass doors. Royce and Petra changed into glinting images of themselves. She saw her own face with its watchful, indrawn expression. Then she looked through the reflections to where empty wicker chairs sat around deserted tables. Only a few weeks ago the glass doors would have been open, guests would have been sitting on the patio. Now there was only darkness.

Jinny stared out more closely, then froze in horror. Her heart pounded in her throat at the suddenness of what she saw. In one of the wicker chairs sat the dark stranger. His long legs were stretched out in front of him, his arms hung down, long-fingered hands brushing the ground. For a second Jinny saw his profile – arched nose, wide, tight-lipped mouth, and blank fall of his face from eye to jaw. Then he turned his head and looked straight at Jinny, stretched out his arm and beckoned to her.

Instantly Jinny swung round in her chair.

'Royce,' she demanded, her voice too loud, bursting through Sally's laughing. 'Do you know the poem about the Border raiders? The one where they come at night and wait at the poet's gate wanting him to ride with them?'

They all turned to look at Jinny, surprised by the tone of her voice, Petra ready to warn her sister to behave herself.

'Even when we were all careering down that mountain I was wondering if you would know it.'

For a moment Royce's face was blank.

'He must know,' Jinny thought. 'He must.'

If Royce knew the poem it would mean that the dark stranger had no power over her; could not make her do what he wanted. Jinny waited, holding her breath, feeling the green eyes staring in at her.

'Got it,' said Royce. 'This is it – "The Raiders" by Will H. Ogilvie.

> "Last night a wind from Lammermoor came roaring up the glen
> With the tramp of trooping horses and the laugh of reckless men
> And struck a mailed hand on the gate and cried in rebel glee:
> 'Come forth! Come forth, my Borderer, and ride the March with me!' " '

'That's it!' cried Jinny and she listened in entranced delight as Royce recited the rest of the poem.

"'I know not if the farms we fired are burned to ashes yet!
I know not if the stirks grew tired before the stars had set!
I only know that late last night when northern winds blew free
A troop of men rode up the glen and brought a horse for me!"'

'I had no idea you possessed such hidden talent,' praised Sally, as everyone at the table burst into applause. People at the other tables joined in, and to Jinny, clapping until her hands burnt, the hotel lounge was real again. It was filled with real living people, their laughter real laughter, and she, Jinny Manders, belonged there. She was one of them. The weird stranger had no claim on her.

Before they left the lounge Jinny screwed up her courage to take another look outside. The wicker chair was empty. There was no sign of the man.

'He must be a tramp,' Jinny thought, driving from her mind the echoes of the sound that had calmed their mounts, of how it would have been if the call had not reached them in time.

Outside there was the sound of footsteps on the gravel path. Jinny turned and fled.

'Wait for me, wait for me,' she cried, catching up with the others, staying close to Petra and Sue as they went upstairs to bed.

CHAPTER SEVEN

Jinny woke early the next morning. Leaving Petra and Sue still asleep, she went down to Shantih. All night she had tossed and turned, half waking from one dream only to sink back into another. Astride Shantih she had galloped from the grim presence of the Water Horse; had dropped down mine shafts only to find the dark stranger there; or had run after Petra and Royce, pleading with them to wait for her. She was in her bedroom at home, and as she had in real life, she was helping Keziah, the old tinker woman, to repaint the Red Horse mural with Keziah's paints. Suddenly Keziah had vanished, leaving her utterly alone.

Jinny flipped down the wide, richly carpeted stairs. She stood waiting, staring about the empty hotel lobby, then went out past the reception desk, through the swing doors to where a smooth lawn reached down to a coven of pines. The moors rose above the hotel grounds to a clear sky that promised a fine day. Jinny thought of Royce; of spending a whole day filming with him.

'Once he really sees Shantih, he's bound to want her in his film,' Jinny thought. 'He could film her galloping over the sands at Finmory.' And Jinny walked with Royce through Finmory, showing him the Red Horse, letting him see her drawings and paintings. She heard his voice asking her to draw pictures for the credits of his film. She imagined herself sitting next to Royce, speeding along the motorway in his scarlet sports car, being driven to London for an art conference. She thought of the way he said her name, making it sound quite different to the way it sounded when other people said it.

Jinny spun round, her long hair shaken out, her eyes sparkling.

'Royce,' she said aloud over the empty hotel grounds.

Then she caught a glimpse of the deserted patio. The wicker chair, where the dark stranger had sat last night watching her through the glass, was empty. Jinny shivered suddenly and hurried on to the field.

While she was greeting Shantih, Brian arrived. Together they fed the ponies, bringing them out of the field two at a time to eat a bucketful of oats and nuts from the sack which Miss Tuke had sent on with Royce. Then they groomed them and Brian boasted about all the riding he had done.

'Should be pretty good this filming lark,' he enthused. 'It'll be something to tell them when I get back to work. Pity about Miss Tuke. Wouldn't have wanted it to happen to her but things have looked up since she departed. Been a bit more life about it.'

'Do you call it "life" getting lost on the moors?' Jinny asked scornfully. 'Shows how much you know about riding on the moors if you think that's life.'

With all her heart Jinny wished that Miss Tuke was still with them. Miss Tuke would have known what to say to any strange men that kept bothering her. If Miss Tuke hadn't hurt herself Jinny could have stayed close beside her and then she would have been quite, quite safe.

Petra and Sue were finishing breakfast when Brian and Jinny got back.

'Thought you'd have come down to help,' Jinny said.

'We knew you'd manage,' said Petra. 'Royce told us to have our breakfast as quickly as possible.'

'They're starting filming at once,' said Sue excitedly. 'One of the extras is waiting to show us the way. Most of them are up there now. We're going to be last.'

'So hurry up,' bossed Petra, toning down her irritation because it included Brian as well as Jinny. 'Get a move on.'

They were filming at a disused croft about half an hour from the hotel. Rounding the corner of the track that led to the croft, Jinny gasped aloud in amazement. It was as if a whole field of folk had dropped from the sky. The ground in front of the croft swarmed with life. There was one large camera on a tripod, and Don, the assistant cameraman, carried a small camera on his shoulder; a man with a long pole with something on the end of it hovered around them; a row of extras dressed as smugglers were sitting on chairs being made up; young men bustled about intent on mysterious errands, and girls with clipboards were imagey and efficient. The whole scene had an air of exclusive excitement. And they were part of it.

Royce, with Sally trotting at his side, came striding across to them.

'What the blazing dickens have you done with those ponies?' he roared. 'I want them filthy not done up like blinking show ponies.'

Jinny gasped in amazement. She had never known her grooming to have such an effect on anyone before.

'That one,' Royce said, pointing to McSporran.

84

'Get him duffed up as quick as you like. I want him for this shot. And get those two ruddy horses out of my sight. Highland ponies, that's all I want.'

Sally said it would have been better not to have brought the horses but that it couldn't be helped now and they would have to leave them in an outhouse at the back of the croft.

'Not yet! Not yet!' roared Royce at a man about to decant a sackful of chickens in front of the croft, and he went dashing across to stop him.

The outhouse had stone walls, a high, raftered ceiling patched with sky and a mud floor.

'Pop them in there,' said Sally, in a tone of voice that was so self-assured no one could have argued with her. 'We'll need you both to cope with the Highlands.'

'She'll be OK with Pippen,' Sue said, knowing what Jinny was thinking.

'That's the way,' said Sally when Pippen and Shantih were both unsaddled. 'Shut them in. Now, Royce wants the brown pony degroomed and standing in front of the croft.'

And almost before she had time to realise what was happening Jinny found herself whisked away to degroom McSporran.

'Mane won't do. Nor the tail,' said Royce, when Jinny presented McSporran.

'Rub bracken into them,' Sue suggested, and together they rubbed bracken and leaf mould into McSporran until he was filthy enough for Royce.

At first Jinny was high with the thrill of it all. To be part of such a glamorous thing as filming blew her up with fizzy excitement. All the people seemed larger than life. They didn't do anything as ordinary as working for their living. They were all part of this crazy, circus world. Jinny watched fascinated as the morning's filming proceeded.

They broke for coffee, served from what looked like a huge furniture van which had been converted into a mobile kitchen.

Royce came across to speak to Petra and Jinny, Sue and Brian, where they waited on the edge of things, each holding two Highlands.

'I want the ponies in the next take. The smugglers will lead them down there. Those two first,' and he pointed to Guizer and Bramble.

'They won't,' stated Jinny. 'Better with Guizer and Juno.'

'Do we have a take-over bid?' sneered Royce. 'Be my guest. A new infant director is in our midst.'

His charm was switched off, his sarcasm was blade sharp.

'I'm only . . .' began Jinny, staggered by the ferocity of Royce's attack.

'Those two next. The white one last and the fawn one in front of him. Now you'll take them across there. Get them into position and the smugglers will take them from you when we're ready to film. Right? When you've given them to the smugglers you keep out of shot. Know what that means?'

'Not really,' Petra smiled. 'Could you explain, please?'

'Best girl at St. Ursula's,' thought Jinny, scowling.

'It means,' said Royce, 'that you keep well away from the blinking cameras. Sweet as you are, darlings, I do not want you in with the smugglers.'

It took Royce ages to decide just where he wanted to take the shots of the smugglers. He moved children, ponies and smugglers here and there over the moor, experimenting with different camera angles until at last he found the right place.

'Silence. No noise, filming,' warned Sally. 'Filming.'

'At flippin' last,' thought Jinny.

The smugglers had hardly taken a step before Guizer swung round and lashed out at Bramble, yanking his rope from the smuggler's nervous hold.

'Cut! Back to your marks everybody,' shouted Royce.

'Told him,' triumphed Jinny silently. 'He'd have listened to Miss Tuke and she'd have told him the same thing.'

They had reached take six before Royce gave in and swopped Bramble for Juno. In two more takes they had the bit of film he wanted.

'It was only because Bramble and Guizer are both boss ponies,' Jinny tried to explain.

'Really?' said Royce, regarding her with total contempt.

'Yes, it's . . .'

'Sally,' Royce roared. 'Get these kids out of my sight!' And he stalked away clutching his clipboard to him.

'Don't annoy him just now,' said Sally.

'I wasn't,' said Jinny indignantly. 'I was only trying to explain . . .'

'Then don't.'

'Just don't say anything,' bossed Petra when Sally left them. 'Can't you see he doesn't want to be bothered with you?'

Jinny stared fixedly over Petra's head, beyond all the commotion of filming.

'Don't blink,' she told herself. 'Blink and they'll see you're nearly crying.' Jinny didn't know why

Royce had turned on her so furiously when he had been so friendly the night before.

'Well don't cry about it,' said Petra. 'You don't think Royce cares twopence about us or the ponies?'

'I'm not crying,' sniffed Jinny, giving in and hunting for a handkerchief, for she *had* thought that Royce cared twopence for her. She had allowed herself to think that Royce cared more than twopence; that he saw her as someone special.

At lunchtime Jinny and Sue brought Shantih and Pippen out into the open again.

'Perhaps you fuss too much about her,' Sue suggested. 'She hasn't minded a bit being inside all morning.'

'Not like her,' said Jinny, watching Shantih grazing calmly at the length of her halter. 'I thought she'd have kicked the walls down.'

'Probably having Pippen with her?'

'Might be,' said Jinny.

Although she didn't like to think about Pippen's behaviour being so much better than Shantih's she preferred it to the only other explanation she could think of. If the man in the black clothes had calmed the ponies yesterday, it would be nothing to him to have settled Shantih today. All morning Jinny had seen no sign of him although she had watched carefully for any glimpse of his dark figure.

The afternoon dragged on. Jinny was so bored that she didn't know what to do with herself. It seemed to take Royce hours to decide how he wanted to film a shot. An old man, who had once farmed around Calmun using heavy horses, had a few lines to say. They had to be broken up into seven or eight words at a time, and even then he got them wrong, over and over again.

'Oh the boredom, the utter boredom,' moaned Jinny, doing funny walks round Fergus and Juno.

At last Royce finished filming the farmer and turned his attention to the ponies. He wanted shots of them loose – grazing, mingling, being themselves.

One of the film crew sprinkled oats over the grass where Royce wanted to film the Highlands.

'Over here,' Sally told them. 'Now take their halters off.'

'But we can't just let them go,' protested Jinny. 'Miss Tuke would never let them loose.'

'That's the way,' said Sally, and before Jinny realised what was happening Sally had lifted Bramble's halter over his ears. 'Let them all go.'

As the ponies searched for the oats Royce danced around them. Hands cupping his face, he darted here and there, seeing camera shots between his hands, organising the filming of each different angle.

'Now for some action,' Royce told them. 'Rouse them up a bit. Get them moving.'

'That's the way, that's the way,' he encouraged. 'More! More! That's what I want. Keep it going. Keep them alight.'

Film crew and extras, all safely out of camera shot, waved arms and jackets and stamped their feet to excite the ponies. One of the film crew threw a handful of earth at Beech's quarters and the pony lashed out with both hind feet. Ponies exploded about him.

'Great! Great! That's it. Again, again,' Royce encouraged between shots.

Jinny supposed that there must be some order about it, but if there was she couldn't see it. It all seemed total chaos to her. Watching the excited ponies, she was glad that Shantih wasn't amongst them. She wouldn't have let anyone throw handfuls of earth at Shantih.

'Once more,' said Royce, 'and it's in the can. I want a low angle shot with the pines behind them.'

The camera whirred, the cameraman shouted, 'Running . . . Speed,' and Royce's voice shouted 'Action!'

After two more takes Sally told them to put the ponies' halters on again, and when at last they had caught the ponies Jinny thought, with relief, that they had finished for the day.

Royce was standing clicking his pen between his teeth, reading half to himself from the typed sheets on his clipboard.

> ' "Garrons bred where the birches cling to the mountain glen,
> Full of the fiery courage they share with the Highland men." '

He looked up and to Jinny's dismay said, 'Now take them up that slope. I want to begin with a long shot of them galloping down to the cameras.'

Following Royce's megaphoned instructions, they climbed the hill dragging unwilling ponies behind them.

'They're as fed up as I am,' Jinny thought. 'They want to pack it in too.'

When Royce was ready to film and the ponies were released they showed no desire to gallop down the hill, only trotting a few paces then stopping to graze.

'They were keen enough to gallop downhill last night,' said Petra, when even reinforcements of chasers from the film crew had failed to produce a downhill charge.

Royce came storming up the hill towards them.

'Doing his director nut,' said Brian, as they waited, holding the ponies by their halter ropes looped round their necks. 'As if it was our fault!'

'Get the brutes moving. Get those ropes off them. Come on, get them woken up.' Royce shouted and swung his arms at Bramble who regarded him with mild amazement and went on grazing.

'They've had enough,' stated Jinny.

Royce ignored her.

'This time send them on downhill. Get at them with the ropes. I want a charge, not a blinking funeral,' and he turned back, racing down to the cameras.

At the next attempt, chased on by swinging halters and showers of earth, the ponies bucked their way downhill but well before they reached the cameras they had slowed to a walk.

Swearing, Royce raced towards them.

'Well catch them!' he yelled. 'Catch the rotters. Blast the Tuke for falling off her horse. She should have been here blinking well organising this. That's what she's getting paid for.'

Sally trotted behind him clutching her clipboard, her stop-watch penduluming from her neck. Behind Sally came another woman with a brightly woven shawl flapping from her shoulders.

'I want a charge. A downhill charge.'

'They'll need to charge to something,' suggested Sally.

'Oats?' said Petra.

'Pippen?' said Sue.

'Shantih?' said Jinny.

By the time Shantih, Pippen and two buckets of oats were established at the bottom of the hill as pony lure and the Highlands were back in their starting place, Royce was beginning to worry about the light.

'This time,' he shouted through his megaphone. 'Let's make it a take first time. Get those oats rustling. Clatter the buckets. Let them know there's food there. Chase them on, up there. You're not in camera and the RSPCA won't see what you're doing. Are you ready? This is it.'

Sue and Jinny rattled their buckets, holding them up so that the Highlands would see them, and Pippen whinnied obligingly. The ponies, chased on by maniacs, careered downhill; snorting, bucking, manes tossing, tails flying about their quarters, they galloped straight at Sue and Jinny, Pippen and Shantih.

Jinny felt the ground reverberating under her feet.

'Ware Guizer,' yelled Sue. 'He's off!'

Jinny saw Guizer had abandonded the charge and was tearing off by himself. Instantly she sprang on to Shantih and galloped to turn him.

'Get back,' Jinny shouted, swooping Shantih round in front of the runaway and turning him back to the others.'

'Near thing,' Jinny shouted triumphantly to Sue, who, still clinging on to Pippen, was surrounded by Highlands fighting over spilled oats, the buckets clattering about their hooves. 'He thought he was off.'

Royce came towards her, rising up on his toes at each step.

'He's going to thank me for catching Guizer,' Jinny thought. 'Thank me for being so quick,' and she smiled down at Royce to show him that she'd completely forgotten how rude he had been to her in the morning.

Royce came right up to Shantih. He stood for a second, staring at Jinny through stone-cold eyes, making her wonder guiltily what she could have done wrong, when she knew she had done nothing, was expecting to be praised.

'You were in shot,' said Royce, firing each word like a bullet.

'What?' exclaimed Jinny, but Royce had already turned on his heel and left.

'You galloped in front of the camera,' Sue explained.

Jinny's heart sank.

'But I had to catch Guizer. He'd have vanished. He could have gone off anywhere. We might never have found him tonight if I hadn't turned him.'

'I think it is *the* sin,' said Sue.

'Sorry, boys and girls. One of the pony kids got into shot. We'll have to take it again.' Royce's megaphoned fury blasted over the moors. 'Everybody back. Shooting it again and make it fast. The light will give us ten minutes at the most.'

'Oh dear,' said Jinny in a collapsed funny voice. 'He is not happy.'

Buckets refilled with oats, Sue and Jinny waited for the Highlands to be released.

'Let them gallop,' prayed Jinny. 'Please God, let them do it right.'

'And this time don't dare move,' said Sue.

'Standing steady,' said Jinny as hooves thundered down towards them, and Guizer, abandoning the herd, high-tailed it out of sight over the moor.

CHAPTER EIGHT

Jinny sat astride Shantih, staring about her at the waves of brackened moorland.

'Guizer,' she yelled. 'Guizer!' But more to hear the sound of her own voice than because she thought there was the slightest chance of Guizer appearing.

'He might, just might have come for Miss Tuke, but never for me,' Jinny thought.

The sun was a sucked lozenge of brilliance firing the undersides of wind-whale clouds into orange, pink and petunia. Already the mountains beyond the moors were featureless; ramparts of night.

'Can't go back without him,' Jinny told herself.

Both Sue and Brian had offered to come with her to help her catch Guizer but Jinny had told them that she could easily catch him by herself; that she would manage better without them getting in her way. Now she wished she hadn't been so independent for these moors weren't the Finmory moors that Jinny knew like a garden. These were strange to her, alien, and now it would soon be night.

When Jinny had first ridden after Guizer she had caught sight of him only a little way ahead. When he saw Jinny and Shantih he had plunged away from them and galloped out of sight behind an outcrop of rock. Jinny rounded the rock to find him grazing. Riding up on Shantih she almost had her hand on him when he sprang out of reach and thundered away. That was the last Jinny had seen of him.

'Guizer!' Jinny yelled hopelessly.

'Can't stay out much longer,' Jinny thought, desperately wishing she had let Sue or Brian come with her. 'Thought I'd only to ride round the hill and I'd find him. Mustn't get caught in the dark. Might not be able to find my way back to the hotel. I might meet . . .'

Hurriedly Jinny urged Shantih on. She didn't dare to think of the strange man in the black clothes. The thought of the Water Horse, in the story she had read at Miss Tuke's, came back to haunt her. How he had changed from Water Horse to dark stranger. He could be waiting to spring out at her from every shadow; be crouching in wait for her by every boulder.

'Shantih,' said Jinny, 'we will ride over the next hill and that is that. If we can't see Guizer then, too bad, concrete Cheddar.'

But Jinny knew she was only kidding herself. You couldn't leave a pony out all night on the moors. If he were to hurt himself in any way, lame himself or wander into one of the treacherous peat bogs, it would be on Jinny's conscience forever. If she couldn't find Guizer herself she would need to go back to the hotel for help.

Shantih breasted through the sea of bracken, rose to the top of a hill and in a hollow, a little way in front of them, was a farmhouse. It was a compact, Monopoly house with four domino windows, a slate roof and a cluster of outhouses. Two haystacks, under tarpaulin mob caps, stood in the corner of a small field next to the farm. Beside one of the stacks a pony was standing helping himself to the hay. A dun pony with a black mass of mane and tail that could only be . . . Was Guizer.

Jinny sighed aloud with relief. She walked Shantih

down to the farm, unknotting Guizer's halter from her waist as she rode. Dismounting, she led Shantih up to the farm. As she reached it, a man came out of a side door.

'Please don't chase him,' Jinny called. 'I've come to get him.'

'So he belongs to you? In that case it's pleased I am to see you for it's the notion he has on him for my hay.'

'I'm sorry he's eating your hay,' said Jinny, 'but I can't tell you how glad I am that I've found him.'

The farmer took Shantih while Jinny advanced on Guizer with an outheld handful of oats.

'Imp of hell,' she said sweetly. 'Cursed of the Lord. Beelzebub.'

Guizer blinked innocent eyes as he walked across to Jinny. He had had enough. It was time to go home. He stood munching oats while Jinny knotted the halter rope round his head.

'I do hope he didn't eat too much hay,' she apologised, leading the captive Guizer back towards the farmer. 'We're filming close to the hotel at Calmun. The Highlands had to gallop loose and he went off.'

The farmer's wife had come to the farmhouse door. Her arms folded over her stretched apron, she watched Jinny without speaking.

'It's the filming she's from,' the farmer said, after he had introduced himself as Mr Muir and the woman as his wife. 'They let the pony away.'

'Och now, the shame of it,' said Mrs Muir, tutting moistly. 'Fancy sending a bit lassie like that over the moors after a beast.'

'I didn't mind,' began Jinny.

'Be leaving them both in the stackyard and in you

come for a wee cup of tea,' continued Mrs Muir, already turning in to the farm.

'Thank you very much,' said Jinny, 'but I can't possibly. I've got to get back to the hotel before it gets dark.'

'It's herself will have the kettle on,' said the farmer as if that settled the matter.

'No,' said Jinny. She knew how long farmhouse teas could take and how impossible it was to escape from them. 'Really no.'

'As if we would be letting you back without a cup,' said Mr Muir scornfully. 'And when you've drunk it I'll be seeing you on to the track for the hotel.'

The smell of newly baked scones drifted through the open farm door.

'Well,' said Jinny. 'I will need to be very quick.'

They left Shantih and Guizer in the stackyard pulling contentedly at the farmer's hay.

'Really I shouldn't,' Jinny told herself as she followed Mr Muir. 'It'll not be this when I'm riding back through the dark.'

'Come away in,' welcomed Mrs Muir and Jinny, stepping into the shadowed kitchen, saw to her dismay a table covered with home baking. It would be half an hour at the very least before she could possibly leave.

'Really, I mustn't stop,' said Jinny, sitting down at the table.

'There now, be helping yourself. It's lucky you are that I was just at the baking,' said Mrs Muir, plying Jinny with treacle scones and farm butter, pouring out strong tea.

An hour later Jinny stood up decisively. 'Thank you very much,' she said firmly. 'That was super. Thank you.'

When the Muirs had discovered that Jinny came from Finmory and knew Mr MacKenzie they had treated her like a long-lost relative. Encouraged, Jinny had told them stories about herself and the old farmer, until, glancing up, she saw to her horror how dark it was outside.

'I remember once,' said Mrs Muir, totally ignoring Jinny's action. 'He went to a sale to buy a horse for the ploughing and back he comes with the beast. Och, the pride of him at the bargain he had, and when they go out to see it, here, was the poor brute not toothless. It was that old not a tooth was left in its head.'

Jinny forced herself across the room to the door. She wanted to stay chatting round the table, wanted to stay where it was safe and warm; to stay with other people. The last thing she wanted to do was ride back over the moors.

'I MUST go,' she said. 'It's almost dark and they'll be getting worried about me.'

'So they will,' said Mrs Muir, reluctantly getting to her feet. 'And them not knowing where you are.'

Out in the farmyard, light from the afterglow of sunset was closing to grey as Jinny, fumbling in her haste, tacked up Shantih.

'I'll walk along with you to put you on the right way,' said Mr Muir. 'It is welcome you would be to leave them here until tomorrow and I'll be taking you over in the car?'

About to mount, Jinny hesitated, She looked round at the darkening night and almost agreed. Then she thought of the fuss there would be tomorrow morning if Royce wanted to film the trekking sequence and Guizer wasn't there.

'It's OK,' she said. 'I'd better get them back tonight.'

'Do not be speaking to the Walker, now,' Mrs Muir called, going back into the security of the farm.

Jinny instantly knew who Mrs Muir meant. He wasn't the Water Horse after all, then. Or was he?

'The Walker? Who's that?' she demanded brightly, trying to sound as if she didn't care particularly.

'No one at all but an old tramp,' said Mr Muir, walking beside Jinny, leading Guizer. 'Sheena had no need to be mentioning him at all. Don't be bothering your head with her nonsense.'

'Does he wear black clothes?'

'You'll have seen him, then? Always the black clothes he has and always at this time of year we see him. Harmless he is, just at the walking. It's no wonder we've given him the name. He can walk over the hill like a young one, yet when my father was a boy they would be seeing the Walker even then. So it is the fair age that is at him.'

'The man I saw had black hair,' said Jinny, shuddering.

'It is the strange thing,' agreed the farmer. 'Not a touch of the snow about him, although when I was meeting him on the hill a year back, you could see it is the old man he is and no mistake about it.'

'I'll say I've changed my mind,' thought Jinny. 'Ask him if I can leave Shantih and Guizer at the farm; ask if he'll drive me to the hotel.'

'Take that track,' said Mr Muir, pointing out the way. 'It is clear enough so you'll have no trouble following it. About half an hour and you'll be out on the road to the hotel. It's an old ruin of a croft you'll be seeing and the next thing you'll be on the road.'

Jinny heard herself thank him, watched herself take Guizer's halter rope, and when all of her was desperate not to leave the farmer, was longing to go back with him to the safety of the farm, she gathered Shantih together and sent her on at a brisk trot along the track.

'You are scared,' thought Jinny, remembering Ken's advice. 'Be scared. This is what being scared is. Let it happen. Be it,' and she rode on through the gathering darkness. The terrors of the moorland at night were all about her. Wind blowing from the mountains carried the beat of the Water Horse's hooves; the Walker crouched unseen, watching, waiting for her approach. But Shantih trotted steadily forward, Guizer keeping pace at her side.

'Not long now,' Jinny told them, the squeak of her voice making the silence more intense. 'We'll soon be back.'

At last Jinny saw the darker mass of the crumbling walls of the croft ahead of her.

'Almost at the road,' she told them, feeling herself relax, for once she reached the road she would be safe.

Shantih, too, seemed to sense the road ahead. She quickened her pace, trotting out with a reaching stride; whiffling to herself as if she, too, would be glad to leave the moorland behind.

'On you go,' Jinny told them and rode forward, her whole being thinking of the lighted hotel and of company.

In the black shadows of the derelict croft something moved. Jinny heard stones being disturbed, the trickle of plaster from the wall, then footsteps, and into the middle of the track came the dark shape of the Walker.

The shock hit Jinny like a tidal wave – absolute, suffocating, blotting everything out except the horror of the fact that what she had been dreading most had happened. She pulled wildly at Shantih's reins, trying desperately to stop her or turn her off the track, but Shantih paid no attention. She had not been hurrying to reach the road. She had known the Walker was waiting for them: had been urgent to reach him.

Shantih carried Jinny right up to the dark figure, and whickering her delight, she pushed her head against his arm.

Jinny had no will left. Her throat was too tight for her screaming to escape, and even if she had been able to scream there was no one to hear her.

The Walker laid a bony hand on Shantih's neck. 'There is no need to be afraid,' he said in a voice of winter. 'I can do you no harm.'

Jinny thought of newspaper headlines, of being found dead on the moor, but more than any of these mundane terrors was the icy dread that the creature who held her there was the Water Horse.

'I come from a friend of yours, from Jo Wilton,' said the Walker, then stiffened suddenly, turning towards the road as a car engine and lights scythed towards them.

They were closer to the road than Jinny had realised. So close that if she screamed it might even be possible for the people in the car to hear her.

For seconds the car lights swung over the Walker. Jinny glimpsed skin as dead as autumn leaves, the arrogant arch of nose, fleer nostrils, jet fall of hair and eyes that shone in the car's headlights with a sea-green glimmer.

The car stopped, and through her screams for help, Jinny heard the door open, a man's voice shouting her name and running footsteps coming towards her. When Mr Muir reached her the Walker had gone.

'It's all right,' Jinny sobbed. 'It's all right.'

'Easy lass,' said the farmer. 'It's safe you are now. There, there. What was at you to have you screaming like that?'

Jinny opened her mouth to say that the Walker had stopped her, but somehow she couldn't tell him, for in the dark figure Jinny had sensed the same strangeness as there was in the Red Horse, had been in the old tinker woman, Keziah; the strangeness that was in herself and Ken but not in Petra or Mike; in Shantih but not in Bramble. The Walker had said that he knew Jo Wilton, and the Wilton Collection had a share of this same magic, making it a sanctuary when Inverburgh Museum, for all its status and respectability, was a graveyard place.

'I got a fright,' said Jinny. 'I thought I heard something moving in the croft,' and she rubbed her eyes, pretending to laugh at herself. 'I didn't realise the road was so close. I expect it was only my imagination.'

'There then,' said Mr Muir, with embarrassed kindness, 'do not be troubling yourself over it. You will not be the first one to panic on the moors at night. Nor the last. It is myself I blame, letting you go off alone with a gossip's talk of a wandering old man in your ears. I could not settle myself until I saw you safe.'

'I'm very glad you came,' said Jinny. 'You've no idea how pleased I am to see you.' But even as she said the words, she knew that they were not totally, completely, absolutely true. Although she had been so scared, in another minute she would have heard what the Walker had to tell her.

'I'll be driving with you to the hotel,' Mr Muir said.

'Honestly,' Jinny protested, 'You don't need to. Now I'm off the moors I'll be quite OK and I expect they'll be looking out for me.'

But the farmer drove slowly ahead of Jinny until they reached the hotel, where he waved out of his car window, wished Jinny good luck with her filming and drove away, almost before Jinny had time to thank him.

On legs that felt like chewed elastic, Jinny watered Shantih and Guizer, gave them a feed and turned them out into the field.

'Typical,' Jinny thought, as the other ponies hardly bothered to lift their heads but went on grazing, paying no attention to Shantih or Guizer. 'They couldn't care less. Just the same as the rest of them. They couldn't care less about me.'

Jinny stomped her way to the hotel, pushed through swing doors, on past the reception desk and clomped upstairs, ignoring the curious stares that followed her progress. Royce and Sally were standing at the top of the stairs. They had obviously changed after their day's filming; looked sleek and bright.

'When they should have been worrying about me. It was bloomin' well Royce's fault, letting ponies gallop about loose,' Jinny thought, and head down, scowling, she made to walk past them.

'Jinny!' cried Royce. 'Jinny darling, where have you been? Don't tell me you've been chasing after that wretched pony all this time?'

Jinny looking up ready to tell Royce in no uncertain terms that that was exactly what she had been doing and that it was all his fault.

Royce's deep blue eyes looked straight at Jinny, concerned and caring about her.

'I had no idea you were still out there. If I'd known I'd have had the whole crew out searching for you. Are you sure you're all right? You look frozen. Anything I can do to help?'

Jinny stood in a haze of sudden happiness.

'I'm fine,' she said.

'Hot bath?' suggested Sally.

'That would be the thing,' said Royce. 'See you bright-eyed and bushy-tailed tomorrow,' and he went on downstairs, turning at the foot of the stairs to smile and wave to Jinny, before he followed Sally through the swing doors.

Jinny gulped, seeing nothing but Royce – his blond hair, his smile – she went on down the corridor to their room.

'Would you look at the state of her!' cried Petra.

Still half blinded by the brightness of Royce, Jinny sat down hard on her bed. She regarded Sue and her sister with a disenchanted eye.

'I would have thought,' she said, 'instead of painting your faces you might have been wondering where I was.'

'You didn't want me to come with you,' said Sue guiltily, a stick of blusher in her hand. 'Petra said you'd be all right as long as you were on Shantih.'

'Did she?' said Jinny, the moment of terror when she had first seen the Walker clear in her mind.

'Well you are, aren't you?' said Petra. 'You're always telling us not to fuss. You think we should be able to read your mind. Worry about you only when you want it.'

Jinny tugged off her filthy jodh boots, dragged off her anorak.

'You'll need to buck up if you're coming down to dinner with us,' said Petra.

'Since you're all so anxious about it, I found Guizer, eventually.'

'Was he OK?' asked Sue.

'Eating a farmer's hay,' said Jinny and collapsed on the bed.

'Not in those disgusting jodhpurs,' said Petra.

'Don't care,' said Jinny.

'Miss Tuke phoned Royce,' Sue told Jinny. 'She's back home. Meant to be resting. Says her head aches a bit and that we must have been crazy to ride down where we did. We should have gone on for another mile then there was a path down to the hotel. That was the steep bit she was worrying about and it's only about half as steep as where we came down. She said she didn't know why we didn't all break our necks.'

Jinny woke with a start. The room was empty. Someone was knocking on the door. In a sudden clutch of fear Jinny lay, hardly breathing.

'Sandwiches and soup,' said a voice outside, and Jinny rushed to open it and take the tray from the maid.

When she had finished eating, Jinny found her sketch pad and pencil, and sitting cross-legged on the bed began to draw.

First she stored snippets of film crew and cameramen, the space around the croft where they had been filming, bustling with activity. She drew Beech bucking when the man had thrown the earth at him, the explosion of ponies around him. Then she drew the charge of Highlands, and then a sketch of the moorland farm, haystacks and Guizer, tiny in a wilderness landscape.

Turning to a clean page, Jinny waited. Secure in

105

the hotel bedroom, she allowed herself to think about the Walker; tried to reach beyond her fears. How had he discovered that she knew Jo Wilton? What had he wanted to tell her? Why did he come every year to walk the moorland ways?

With precise, sure lines, Jinny drew his gaunt face, his bleak, angular body. Then she drew Shantih and the Walker as she had seen them from Lillybank's window. Whoever he might be, Shantih trusted him.

When Petra and Sue came back, giggling together, Jinny was in bed. She shut her eyes, pretending to be asleep.

'Nearly forgot to tell you,' said Petra, 'Royce wants to film Shantih.'

Jinny sat bolt upright. 'Wants to film Shantih!' she echoed in delight.

'It was when he saw you galloping after Guizer. He wants some shots of her with the moors as a background.'

Jinny saw Shantih flaunting, silken, against the rough texture of the moors, the grandeur of the mountains.

'I knew he would,' she sighed.

'He wants me to lead her up and down,' said Petra, and she took what looked like a net curtain from the pile that Sue was carrying. She began to arrange it round her shoulders and because they were Petra's shoulders the white curtain draped itself around her in instant glamour. 'I'm to wear these, pinned together into a kind of floaty gown.'

'You what?' cried Jinny.

'And Shantih has to prance at my side. My side, not yours.'

106

CHAPTER NINE

'She's my horse,' stated Jinny. 'And no one is going to lead her except me.'

'Jinny darling,' said Royce. 'I understand exactly how you feel about it.'

'You don't,' said Jinny, 'or you wouldn't have suggested that Petra should lead her.'

Surrounded by Petra, Sue, Brian, Sally, Pippen and eight Highlands, Jinny and Royce faced each other. They had all just arrived at the location for the day's filming. Four of the extras were being transformed into Royce's idea of pony trekkers. A tall, Sloane Ranger type was to ride Pippen, taking the part of the trek leader. But before the trekking sequence, Petra, dressed in white robes, was to be filmed leading Shantih.

'Believe me, I do understand. No one understands possession more than I do. Now come down from Shantih and let us discuss it like two reasonable human beings.'

Reluctantly Jinny dismounted.

'Petra is not leading her,' she said, feeling instinctively that Royce had won the first round by getting her to dismount.

'There,' said Royce. 'That's better.' He smiled at Jinny, charming, manipulating – certain that in a few more minutes he would get what he wanted.

'I'll explain it to you. While the credits are being run each part of the series will open and close with a montage of quick shots of many different aspects of the horse. I have film of a girl, remarkably like Petra, but not in the least like your sweet self. She is dressed absolutely correctly in a black jacket, boots, bowler – the lot – and she's schooling a chestnut dressage horse. I want shots of Petra – dramatic, mythical – white gown flowing about her, Shantih's mane and tail billowing out, with the backdrop of the mountains behind them. I'm going to cut this into the schooling sequence. One second we see the formal, the limiting, the striving for precision and control; the next, the myth, the subconscious dream, the inward vision.

Royce spoke directly to Jinny. At first she tried not to listen to him, knowing that no matter what he said it was all aimed at one result – to make her give in and let Petra lead Shantih. Yet, despite herself, Jinny was caught in the enchantment of Royce's vision. Without having words to express it, Jinny knew the need to control and by controlling try to keep things safe. She knew, too, the other force, wild and dangerous that always tugged at her heart.

'So you see you must let Petra lead her.'

'She's my horse.'

'This once?'

'Oh Jinny, stop causing such a fuss,' declared Petra. 'I'm not going to harm her. It's not as if I'm going to swim her across a loch or jump her over a five-bar gate. I'm not even going to ride her, only lead her.'

Jinny glowered at her sister. 'I hate you,' she thought. 'Hate you. Not only do you come pushing in where you're not wanted on *my* thing, but you bloomin' well steal Sue away from me. Sue was my friend before you came butting in, and now, all this week, she's hardly spoken to me. All because of you.

108

You're always bloomin' well there, spoiling my life. And I'm supposed to hand Shantih over to you and say nothing.'

'Jinny,' said Royce, putting his arm round her, drawing her to him.

'For me?' He smiled at her – elegant, sophisticated, charming – and Jinny knew she was going to give in.

'Well it's not fair,' she said lamely. 'And I don't see why Petra should, because Shantih is my horse. If Petra gets kicked don't blame me,' and grudgingly, Jinny handed Shantih's reins to Royce.

'Hallelujah!' said Petra. 'What a fuss about nothing.'

'Don't forget she's an Arab,' said Jinny, turning on her heel, beginning to walk away from the group. 'A pure-bred Arab not a hand-knitted Highland.'

'Don't go,' called Royce. 'We need you to help us.'

Jinny ignored him. Without looking round, she plodded resolutely on. When she did turn round she was far enough away to be able to watch the filming as if she were sitting in a theatre, staring down at actors and actresses not Royce or Petra or Shantih.

'Always Petra,' thought Jinny. 'All my life she's been there. Doing everything better than I can. Being the pretty one, the clever one. Always smarming up to people. Always clean and smart. And now she's got Shantih as well!'

Jinny stared in disgust, watching them fit medieval reins with embroidered hangings on to Shantih's bridle. She watched until Petra came out of the TV van wearing her long white robe, caught at the waist with a silver chain.

'Bloomin' Petra,' Jinny said aloud, and she walked

109

on up the hillside and round a rocky scree so that she could no longer see the filming. Film crew, cameras, ponies, Shantih and Petra had vanished. The peace of the hills lay all about her.

At last she sat down on a boulder. Elbows on her knees, chin propped on her fists, she stared into hazy distance. A burn raced over stones, chattering to itself; a heron flapped with lazy wingbeats, crossing the mountains in its own solitude, and the voice of the Walker spoke at her side.

'This time you will listen to me.'

Jinny startled to her feet. Sitting on the ground close beside her was the Walker. He was leaning back on one elbow, lank legs crossed in front of him, bony hands spread out in the heather. He stared up at Jinny, his head angled, questing the air like a blind hound, uncertain of the scent.

'There is no need to be afraid. Listen to your true self and you will know that you are not afraid.'

The green eyes of the Walker held Jinny's gaze.

'You who were chosen to find the Horse god; you who know the power of the Red Horse; who released the fire horse from the death of stone and ice; you who serve must be beyond fear.'

Mesmerised, Jinny stared down at the Walker. With his words she felt the reality of her everyday world floating from her, as if the doors of a prison opened on to vistas of freedom, and she stepped out into a world of shimmering beauty, a world at once magnetic and terrifying, that spoke so clearly to her inner being that its very strangeness was a homecoming.

'Jo Wilton is one of us. You trust him, trust me.'

The Walker reached forward, touched Jinny's arm with his claw hand.

110

'Listen with care,' he said. 'We have little time. Already they are looking for you. Tomorrow, before dawn, you are to come with me to witness the Dance of the Golden Horses. They only dance on one morning in the year. Tomorrow is that morning. Every year I am there. This year you are to come with me. You must come of your own free will. I cannot force you.'

His grip tightened on Jinny's arm, the withered face stared up at her.

'It was not always so. Once I had the power,' the Walker whispered through the lipless slit that was his mouth. 'But now you are free to choose.' The drift of autumn leaves was in his voice.

'Who are you?' demanded Jinny. 'What dance? Where is it? Why have I to see it?' and as she spoke she heard Sue's voice calling her name and heard the beat of galloping hooves.

'Be at the clump of pines beyond the hotel wall by four in the morning. I will be there. You must come alone. Tell no one.'

'Jinny!' cried Sue, tugging Pippen to a halt, ignoring the Walker. 'Someone's going to be hurt if you don't get back to Shantih at once. She's going daft. She must know you're up here. She's going crazy to get to you.'

'Fire horse,' breathed the Walker. 'Ride the fire horse.'

Breaking from the Walker's spell Jinny went with Sue.

'You weren't talking to that weirdo, were you?' asked Sue as Jinny looked back.

The Walker was standing on the far side of a burn, his black hair blowing about his head, his body poised on the edge of movement, his face lifted, luminous green eyes staring after Jinny.

'Free to choose,' echoed his voice in Jinny's head. 'Choose . . . Choose . . .'

'Come on,' urged Sue. 'Do hurry up. Petra's nearly in tears and that'll ruin her make-up.'

Running at Pippen's side Jinny saw Shantih rearing straight up. Two extras were hanging on to her reins while Petra watched nervously from a safe distance, her face painted into a mask of green and silver.

'Whoa, whoa the horse,' cried Jinny. 'Oh, steady the horse. Steady Shantih.' She ran with low strides to where the Arab stood quivering, goggle-eyed, staring up the hillside, not at Jinny but beyond her.

Jinny took Shantih's reins, and scowling about her said, 'I told you she wasn't a Highland. I told you I should have led her. She's my horse not Petra's.'

'Get on with it,' said Royce. 'You're not here on a blinking Sunday School picnic, you know. Take her over to that rock. Now, Petra darling, running at her side, the way I showed you.'

Cameras whirred and Petra ran at Shantih's side while the Arab, head high, hooves springing from a molten earth, plunged and fretted.

Jinny heard only the Walker's words. 'Choose. Choose. Free to choose.' Saw more clearly than Petra or Shantih the green, translucent eyes of the Walker. Felt his hand bite into her arm.

'To go out at night alone, to meet him?' Jinny shuddered, clutched her arms about herself.

'Tell no one. Come alone,' his voice commanded in Jinny's head. It was as though at the back of the Walker stood a great black horse and it was the horse's whinny that carried the words that drifted into Jinny's mind.

For another six shots Jinny reorganised Shantih,

handed her back to Petra, who was filmed running at her head.

'That's it, dear,' Royce praised, satisfied at last. 'Just what I wanted. Well done. Well done.'

He smiled at Jinny. 'Not too painful?' he asked, but she was hardly aware of him.

'Break for coffee,' Royce called, magnanimous, having total control over his kingdom.

It was after lunch before he was ready to film the trekking sequences. Jinny was to ride Bramble, while Shantih was shut away in the same outhouse as she had occupied yesterday. When Jinny left her she stood calmly, making no attempt to escape.

'She knows,' thought Jinny. 'She's waiting for tonight.' But how could Shantih know? How could she?

CHAPTER TEN

From where she lay in bed, Jinny could see the luminous hands of Petra's travelling clock. It was almost half-past one. In two hours Jinny would have to get up and dress without disturbing Petra or Sue. Then creep through the sleeping hotel out into the night where Shantih waited for her; where the Walker waited.

That was if she went out at all. For Jinny knew that she had only to pull the bedclothes over her head, curl up telling herself all the commonsense reasons why she most certainly should not go out to meet the Walker, and the next thing it would be morning. She could forget all about it; could tell herself how sensible she had been; what a ridiculously dangerous thing it would have been to have gone out with the Walker. This could be her choice – to stay safe and secure; to choose not to know.

Jinny looked at Petra's clock. Its bright and crazy hands had taken a quantum leap forward. Now it was five past two. Jinny stared hard at it. When she kept her eye on it the hands hardly moved at all.

Who was the Walker? If he was only a tramp how did he know Jo Wilton? How had he managed to stop the ponies from charging down to Calmun? Jinny heard again the low, sweet sound that had calmed the ponies. It had been close to the sound that Shantih made when she saw Jinny unexpectedly – a trembling flutter of sound.

When Shantih trusted the Walker surely Jinny

could as well. She would go with him to see the Dance of the Golden Horses. The words filled Jinny's mind with pictures; glinting, half-seen pictures of a dream world where riderless, golden palomino horses danced with the stately, controlled grace of the Spanish Riding School stallions; danced for herself and the Walker.

'Jennifer Manders,' Jinny told herself, sitting bolt upright, speaking silently, severely, inside her head. 'What would your parents say?'

The thought deflated Jinny's dream. She knew her parents would be horrified at the thought of her going out alone at night to meet a stranger. She knew that they would totally forbid her to go. If the Walker wanted her to see the Golden Horses why hadn't he come into the hotel and discussed it with Royce and Petra? Why had he always wanted to speak to her alone? The whole idea of going out to meet him was totally ridiculous. Of course she couldn't go. Couldn't possibly go.

And yet, not to go was impossible as well. The Walker had spoken of Shantih as the fire horse and had known about the Red Horse mural. He had even known how Jinny had rescued Shantih from the snow-covered Finmory moors, when she had found Shantih lying injured by the standing stones. 'You who released the fire horse from the power of stone and ice.'

Impossible not to go: impossible to go. Jinny sat staring at the clock, transfixed by the snail-trail of its luminous circling.

'Choose,' demanded the Walker's voice. 'Free to choose.'

But Jinny could not. The more she thought about it, the more impossible it became to make a decision.

Impossible to be so foolish as to go. Impossible to be so foolish as not to go.

Once Petra turned restlessly and Jinny thought that she would wake her sister, tell her everything and that would be that. If Petra knew about it there would be no danger of Jinny having to go out alone into the night. But the temptation was like a first snowflake, dissolved almost before it had taken shape.

By three o'clock Jinny still had no idea what she was going to do. Her brain was clenched tight. Her thoughts chased each other in ever narrowing circles. She was lying murdered on the hillside. She was with the Walker in a high place, was filled with a joyous anticipation as the Golden Horses came, proud-stepping towards them. But no way between the two impossibilities.

'If only Ken were here,' Jinny thought hopelessly. 'He would know what I should do. Or if Jo Wilton were here. If he could tell me that he really does know the Walker and that I can trust him.'

And the obvious solution clicked into Jinny's mind. She could phone Jo Wilton.

Jinny jumped out of bed. She gathered up her clothes, crossed to the door, her feet absorbing the carpet as she eased them into it. At the door she put down her pile of clothes, clattering a jodh boot against the skirting board, then she eased the door knob in her hands and inched the door forward. On the other side she gathered her clothes to her, then, holding her breath, she closed the door again. For moments Jinny stood listening, but the regular breathing behind the door remained unchanged.

Jinny dashed for a bathroom. She dressed with clumsy fingers, expecting that every minute would bring an outraged Petra to bang on the door, demanding what Jinny was up to now. She went along the corridor, down the broad staircase to the hotel lobby. A dim light burned at the reception desk but, to Jinny's relief, there was no sign of any of the hotel staff. She crossed to the public telephone, switched on the light above it and opened the directory to find the number of the Wilton Collection. For a moment she paused, her hand on the receiver, aware of the listening hotel pressing down about her; of Jo Wilton, sleeping but in seconds to be jarred awake by the alarm of a phone ringing in the night; aware too of Shantih, and the Walker waiting in the dark of the hills. Jinny swallowed hard and concentrated totally, as she dialled the Wilton's number.

She heard the phone ring out and waited. At first impatiently, desperate to hear Jo Wilton's voice and then with a cold despair as the inhuman, mechanical sound went on and on.

Jo Wilton wasn't there or he wasn't going to answer. If he didn't answer would she go? 'Twenty-five, twenty-six, twenty-seven,' Jinny counted the rings, telling herself that Jo Wilton was an old man, it would take him a while to reach the phone. But he had to come. He must come.

'Thirty, thirty-one, thirty-two. Please let him be there,' prayed Jinny. 'He must be there. He must.'

It wasn't a book she was reading. It was real, and she knew that much as she might want to, she would never go out to meet the Walker without some proof of his integrity.

'Answer, oh answer,' she pleaded.

The crackle of the phone being lifted shocked through Jinny like electricity, as if it had been the last thing she had been expecting.

'Hallo,' and although the voice sounded as if it travelled from the other side of the moon, it was Jo Wilton.

Jinny fed money into the phone.

'It's Jinny here,' she said. 'Terribly sorry! I'm at Calmun being filmed with Miss Tuke's ponies. There's an old man in black clothes who says he knows you. I'm meant to be meeting him now. That's why I'm phoning to find out . . .'

Jo Wilton's calm voice cut through Jinny's high, nervous chatter.

'You were right to phone,' he said. 'You do not need to be afraid. You must go with him. He has proof of . . .' and Jo Wilton's words were lost in the noise of the pay-tone.

Jinny scrabbled in her pocket, feeling her drawing pad and pencil but she had no more money. It didn't matter – she had heard enough.

She went out through the swing doors and stood staring into the darkness. Moving clouds gave the illusion of a travelling moon, yet the dense blackness of the trees was still. It was a wind of the upper air. Cautiously Jinny made her way down to the ponies' field. Shantih was waiting at the gate, gazing towards the hotel, as if she was expecting Jinny.

For a moment Jinny clutched her arms round Shantih's neck, felt the strong security of her horse, pressed her face against her.

'Shantih,' she whispered. 'Shantih.'

But the Arab tossed her head impatiently. Shattering the night silence with a clarion whinny, she broke away from Jinny to circle the field with a tornado of hoofbeats before she returned to the gate. Surging against it with violent urgency, she sent her cry of frustration winging out through the

118

darkness towards the darker mass of the pine trees.

Jinny had left Shantih's bridle hidden beneath the hedge. Finding it she slipped the reins over Shantih's head and let her through the field gate.

'Steady, steady,' she cried. 'Go easy, easy now.'

Although every fibre of Shantih's being was charged with her desire to reach the Walker, she stood perfectly still while Jinny bridled her, gathered up her reins and leapt on to her back. Then, as surely as she knew the way from Finmory House to the sea, Shantih made her way to the windbreak of pines, where the Walker waited. Her trot was high as a dressage horse's piaffe, elevated, raised, triumphant.

The Walker moved from the dense blackness of the pines, and Jinny panicked. He was not the Walker. He was the Water Horse. For a second the two images merged in her mind. The Water Horse, created by the horror story, and the Walker, black mane, green eyes and a voice that spoke in a secret, whinnying speech.

Jinny yanked at Shantih's reins, kicked wildly trying to turn her and gallop away from this night terror. Her heart battered in her throat, her hard hat crammed with a vice-like tension around her head. It was a trap and she had come blundering into it. The Walker was mad. He had not had the power to make her come but she had come all the same. Frantically Jinny fought to turn her horse but Shantih was totally unaware of her rider. She knew only one end – to be with the Walker. Jinny was helpless.

'You have come,' said the Walker. His voice carried neither praise nor blame, pleasure nor condemnation. He laid his hand on Shantih's neck and with the other hand he took something from his pocket.

'Jo Wilton gave me this,' he said. 'In case you were afraid. So that you should know I am one of you.'

He held his hand out to Jinny, giving her the object he had taken from his pocket. Jinny's hand closed on a small nugget of metal and instantly she knew what it was.

The Walker had given her the little statue of the Horse god she had found buried on the moors. He must have brought it from the Wilton. It lay sweet and solid in Jinny's hand. She saw again, in her mind's eye, the tail kinked over the little statue's back, the delicate, dished, Arab face, its goggle eyes and wide nostrils. And with the reality of the statue came the reality of the Celtic Horse god rearing over the altar; the reality of the Red Horse Jinny had experienced in dreams.

'Now,' whispered the Walker. 'Leave your fear behind.'

Jinny's doubts and fears vanished. She rode to the Dance of the Golden Horses. The Walker moved at her side, keeping pace with Shantih. They crossed the moor without following any track, yet moving true and direct like gulls crossing an evening sky.

'Who are you?' Jinny demanded. It seemed the one question she had to ask. If she knew who the Walker was, other things would fall into place.

'They call me by my true name. I am a walker. I walk the ancient, forgotten ways and by my walking I keep them open for a future time. I serve the Masters.'

The harsh, rusty voice mingled with the tread of Shantih's hooves, the clink of her bit, the night breath of the moors, the roaring silence of the mountains and the wind howling far above human hearing. It was the voice that spoke in Jinny's own heart, telling her things she had always known but had never remembered before.

'Each line of power leads to a holy place; a place of wholeness. This land is in the keeping of the Horse spirit. This way leads to the Dance of the Golden Horses. Once in a year they dance. The energy of the dance holds the worlds, cat's cradle, in its weaving.'

'What dance? What is the dance?'

'You ride to experience.'

'But why me?'

At Jinny's side the Walker threw back his head and laughed, mocking, sardonic. His eyes glinted green. His hand laid on Shantih's shoulder controlled the Arab, not Jinny's riding.

'I cannot tell you yet, but the time will come when you will understand,' he said. 'Always I have walked this Way alone, yet at this turning, I must take you with me; a girl so unaware she would cling to those who sleep, rather than dare to wake.'

The substance of the night faded, grew thin. There was no light yet, only a certainty of light to come. Jinny had lost all sense of direction. She had no idea where the hotel was, she had left it behind, as she had left Petra and Sue, sleeping.

The horizon was edged about them, a tight hem-stitching that held the earth secure in the immensity of space. Space that grew luminous as all life waited for the coming of the sun.

'This is the place,' breathed the Walker, and Shantih stopped without any word from Jinny.

There seemed to be some kind of mound in front of them. Peering through the grey light Jinny could make out the rising smoothness of the ground in front of her, unnatural in the rugged moorland.

121

'She will wait here,' the Walker said as Jinny dismounted, and he stretched forward to breathe slowly into Shantih's nostrils. 'Now come.'

Jinny followed him round the base of the mound until they came to a boulder set in the side of the mound. The Walker grasped it, and as Jinny watched the boulder swung outwards revealing the entrance to a tunnel.

'We enter a holy place,' the Walker said, and stooping down, he led the way from the outer world to the inner.

Without hesitation Jinny followed him. Her old world of family and friends was left behind. The tunnel they walked along was too low for Jinny to stand upright. She walked crouching. Beneath her feet were slabs of stone, and the walls, which she could touch with her outstretched hands, were also of stone. The boulder which the Walker had moved from the tunnel entrance had swung back into place and it was too dark to allow Jinny to see the carvings on the tunnel walls. But she was able to trace the raised designs with her fingers, to see blindly the horses carved on the walls; to feel the arch of a proud neck, the strength of a back and plunging hoof.

They went on until they reached the end of the tunnel. In the darkness Jinny could sense the space about her. The pressure of the Walker's hand on her shoulder told her to wait. She sat cross-legged, without moving, conscious of the Walker seated by her side.

High above them a beam of light pierced the darkness, for a second-arrow sharp, but instantly lost in its own diffusion. It grew stronger and the darkness began to swim into light. Light that grew steadily more powerful until Jinny could see that she was sitting at the entrance to a cave.

The light drew shadows from the roughness of the cave walls. Shadows that linked and grew to form the shapes of horses. A shiver of delight ran through Jinny as she watched the horses rise out of the walls of the cave. Then she saw that she had not been the first to see horses on the cave walls, for where the horses were, someone had traced their outlines. Not imposing them on to the walls of the cave but easing them out of the stone itself; taking the spirit that was already there and giving it flat, two-dimensional form.

The light grew stronger. Colour flamed from the rock. In orange and yellow and scarlet the horses painted on the cave walls burnt chestnut gold. Brimming with excitement Jinny stared about her, twisting her head to see the horses rearing and bucking all around her.

The Walker drew in his breath, sharp and sudden, as the sun's rays filled the cave, and in that light the Golden Horses were freed from the stone. They danced, brilliant soaring creatures of air and fire. They were Shantih and the Red Horse, were the shapes of the Celtic horse god, yet their dance was beyond physical movement. Lifted out of the confines of her body Jinny danced with them in a timeless ecstasy of joy.

Slowly the light withdrew and Jinny stared again through eyes that limited her vision, would not let her see. The cage of her bones closed her in. Yet before the light faded completely she was aware of the horses exactly as they were painted on the walls of the cave. The artist in her knew their precise line and colour. Her hand and arm knew of themselves the exact movements that had given the spirit of the horses two-dimensional form so many thousands of years ago.

Once more aware of the Walker, Jinny sat on in silence. When she stood up she followed him into the tunnel. What had happened in the cave she hardly knew. Only that her whole world would never be the same again.

Out on the hillside Shantih, waiting where she had been left, turned mild, incurious eyes at their return. The Walker left Jinny without a word or a backward glance. She leant against Shantih watching him as he moved wind-swift through the waves of bracken, until he disappeared from her sight. Her arm over Shantih's neck, scratching at the roots of her mane, Jinny gazed over the moorland at a world newly created, at colour more brilliant than she had ever seen before.

Hearing the sound of hooves, she swung sharply round and saw Royce, leading Heather, coming towards her.

'So this is where you are!' he said. 'Where the devil did you disappear to?'

CHAPTER ELEVEN

Royce's voice reached Jinny from another world. She could only stand and stare at him. Almost, she did not know who he was, had never known him.

'Royce', she exclaimed in dismay. The sound strange in her ears. Her own voice no longer part of herself.

'Well, what have you been up to?'

Jinny had no reply. She could hardly understand the question.

'Come on, out with it. What on earth are you doing up here at this time in the morning? I feel responsible for you kids, with Auntie Tuke out of action. Got to keep an eye on you.'

Jinny struggled back to the world she had left when she went into the cave. The world where filming was real; ponies were real; where the sound 'Calmun Hotel' meant the place where she was staying. Jinny screwed up eyes and mind, forcing herself back to the world she had almost forgotten; back to where Royce was a film director. Jinny looked at him again and saw him once more as she had known him – charming, sophisticated, someone who said her name in a special way, who knew her favourite poems as well as she did.

'Where have you been? I couldn't sleep. Came out for a breath of early morning air, thought I'd give the sun a shock. Then the notion took me to ride one of the ponies. Take it up the hills and see what the light would be like up there for some dawn filming. I'm luring this beast to me when it struck home that her ladyship was missing. I was dashing back to rouse you when I decided that I couldn't face the trauma so early in the day and that it was unlikely she would have strayed far from the others. So I set off to find her myself. I'd more or less given up all hope of tracking her down and was enjoying the ride when this creature heard another horse. Took off towards it, and there's Shantih standing like a blinking statue on the moor, and bridled, so I knew you must be here too!'

Jinny stared at him, saying nothing.

'I hung around knowing you would be coming back for her, but no sign of you. I'm leading this creature up and down, composing letters to your dear parents, informing them of their daughter's disappearance, when I look round and you're back. Instant Jinny! So let's have it. Where were you?'

'I . . . We . . .' stuttered Jinny.

'You weren't here, then you were. You didn't appear from thin air so where did you come from? Thick ground?'

'I was only riding Shantih,' said Jinny desperately, saying the first thing that came into her head; the only excuse she could think of. 'And I had to spend a penny. That's all.' She couldn't bear to think what would happen if Royce were to discover the cave. 'Hadn't we better get back. They'll be ready to start filming.'

'Some penny, more like fifty pence the time you were away. I've been hanging about here for ages,' said Royce, taking in Jinny's anxious expression, her blurted excuses, her anxiety to be back at the hotel. 'Filming starts when I say, so there's no panic. Where were you?' He looked round carefully.

'There's something odd about this part of the moor. That mound looks to me as if it were a Stone Age burial mound.'

'No it's not,' said Jinny. Then, realising that she had sounded far too definite, she added, 'Least it doesn't look like one to me, and I don't care what you're doing, I'm going back for some breakfast.'

'Not so fast,' said Royce. 'You do know something, don't you? Something you don't want me to find out,' and he moved quickly to Jinny's side and grabbed hold of Shantih's bridle.

'Of course not. You're talking nonsense.'

Royce examined the mound from his new viewpoint.

'Talking nonsense, am I?' he exclaimed, his voice brightening. 'I was right. Out of thick ground!'

In seconds he had leapt up the mound to where he had spotted the trampled bracken around the boulder. He knelt in front of it, tugging, pulling and suddenly the stone moved. Jinny, abandoning Shantih, raced up to him.

Royce was crouching at the mouth of the tunnel. From his hand a pocket torch sent a weak beam of yellow electric light spilling over the carved walls of the tunnel.

'Lord, what a find!' he shouted. 'What a blinking, miraculous find.' His face shone with enthusiasm, his voice echoed in the long-silent tunnel. 'How did you find it? Why didn't you want to tell me about it?'

Royce did not wait for answers. He went on down the tunnel, shouting out with excitement as he went.

'Never been anything like this in Scotland before. They always suspected that there might be, but this is the first one that's been discovered,' he cried. 'Look at that head! It is incredible!'

Jinny followed, stumbling behind him until he came to the cave, and there even Royce was silent. He strode into the middle of the floor, shining his torch about him, but its fading beam was too weak to do more than show glimpses of the painted walls. Royce sprang back up the tunnel, grabbing Jinny by the arm.

'We've got to get back to the hotel,' he yelled. 'Bring lights up here so we can see it. It's marvellous, utterly marvellous. Stone Age or something like that. Don't know enough myself but once the experts get up here they'll know. Be crawling over each other to see it.'

Jinny allowed herself to be pulled along to the entrance of the tunnel. Her mind still dazzled by the vision of the dancing horses, she felt the horror of Royce's words as if they were pressed, burning, against her nerves. He had no right to come into this place, shouting, loud, without reverence. What experts did he mean? Who was he going to tell about the cave?

'Now,' said Royce when they were outside again, 'there are some decent torches in the van. I'll bring them up and then we'll see what's really there.'

'You can't!' cried Jinny. 'You mustn't tell anyone. Not ever. You shouldn't have seen the cave. You must promise never to tell anyone about it. It's not just a cave, it's something more.'

'I should think it blinking well is something more. It looks to me like the find of the century. Once the news breaks there'll be thousands flocking up here to see it. And glory, what a film it will make!'

'You mustn't film it. You mustn't tell anyone. It's a secret, special, magic place. No one must know about it.'

'Look here sweetheart, everybody is going to know about this. They're going to know how you and I found it. I read up on painted caves for the film, and believe you me, there is nothing like it in Britain. You don't unearth a place like that and sit on it. It's a great discovery.'

'No! No it's not. It's a holy place. You should never have seen it.'

'Oh, just for yourself, is it?' said Royce, laughing at Jinny. He was sparkling with excitement at his find, keen to be galloping back to the hotel, to be telling people about it.

Jinny stared frantically up at him. Once he reached the hotel and told everyone about the cave it would be too late. They would come back with lights; phone archaeologists to poke and pry; bring television cameras; and the image of the cave would be spilt out on to a billion screens. Crowds would come to stare at it; voices, loud and ignorant, would desecrate the silence; they would stamp cigarette ends into the floor; leave behind them a litter of plastic wrappers and deface the walls with graffiti. The thought clawed at Jinny, twisted her with physical pain. She had no words to share her experience of the dancing horses with Royce; no way of telling him what she knew intuitively – that if he told the world about the cave its spirit would be lost for all time, the power that it contained would vanish. The Golden Horses would never dance again.

'You can't,' she cried. 'You mustn't.'

'Darling, I can and I must.'

Clutching for ways to tell him why the cave had to remain secret, sealed, Jinny said, 'It would be like selling Shantih back to the circus.'

'It would be what?'

'You know,' pleaded Jinny. 'Like the Arab selling his horse for gold. You understood the poem. You knew what it meant.'

'That rubbish,' said Royce. 'We'd an English master at my prep school who forced us to learn reams of that stuff. That's the only reason I can vamp it up today.'

His words slapped Jinny across the face. How had she ever been so stupid as to be taken in by him? All the time he had been laughing at her. Petra had been right again.

'Come on, now,' cajoled Royce. 'Here we are with something so special it is going to blast the headlines, and you stand there looking like Little Orphan Annie. Jinny dear, come on,' And Royce tried to put his arm round her and draw her to him but Jinny flung furiously away.

'Very well, sulk if you want. I'm going back to the hotel.' Royce strode off to retrieve Heather from where she was grazing.

Grasping Shantih's reins, Jinny stood without moving.

'You won't find it again,' she yelled. 'You'll never find your way back to it.'

'I will,' promised Royce, swinging himself on to Heather. 'Sorry to disappoint you but I have what's called in hunting circles "an eye for a country". Be seeing you.' And he kicked Heather into a trot, riding, sure of his way, straight to the hotel.

Hot, angry tears poured down Jinny's cheeks. She stared helplessly after Royce. There was nothing she could do to stop him. In an hour, two hours, he would be back bringing other people with him and then it would be too late. The world would know. The destruction of the cave would be sure to follow.

'He can't,' Jinny cried to Shantih. 'Can't. There must be some way of stopping him.'

But by herself there was no way Jinny could stop Royce. Her only hope was to find the Walker.

Jinny sprang on to Shantih. 'Find him, Shantih,' she whispered to her horse. 'Find the Walker.'

Jinny urged Shantih into a gallop, plunged recklessly through knee-deep bracken and snares of wiry heather. She had only the faintest idea where the Walker might be. She knew the direction he had taken over the moor but nothing more. Recklessly she urged Shantih on, but the rolling moorland stretched about her in deserted waves, was featureless, held no dark shape.

Loose stones clipped under Shantih's hooves as she stumbled, half fell, recovered. But Jinny never slackened her flying speed. As she crested each height of moorland she was certain she must see the Walker, but when her eyes met only the reaching emptiness, she hardly paused before plunging downhill to ride on to the next vantage point.

She had lost all sense of time or direction. Only to ride, to find the Walker. Only to stop Royce going back to the cave. If she did not find him soon it would be too late. As she rode, Jinny looked desperately about her, her searching as driven as the speed she demanded from Shantih.

'Must find him,' she cried, silent and inward. 'Must find him before it's too late.'

At last she slowed Shantih down and turned her head into the wind to ease her bellows-breath. Standing in her stirrups Jinny sent her voice, with its plea for help, winging into space. Again and again she cried out to the Walker for help. It seemed as if the moors took her words and carried them onwards, spreading the sound, swooping and searching for the Walker.

Suddenly Shantih wheeled round, stood motionless, then, with a thunderous whinny, plunged to meet the dark figure coming towards them.

Mesmerised by the glare of the Walker's green eyes, Jinny blurted out her story. She saw fury brim and overflow, distorting the Walker's features. For a dread moment she thought he would turn on her, drag her down from Shantih and trample her in his rage, but he only laid his hand on Shantih's bridle.

The sound of his agony and regret that followed Jinny's words was lost in the fury of the speed that carried them back to the cave. In the blinding force of their ride Jinny, hanging on to Shantih, did not know whether the Walker raced at Shantih's side; whether he rode astride a gaunt, black horse or whether there was only the horse itself – the pits of its nostrils scarlet with blood, blue-black mane slimed with weed storming about its bony skull; the green eyes blazing and its razor-sharp hooves daggering the earth with violence.

As the mound came into sight, Jinny saw Heather and Beech standing grazing and, to her dismay, Royce and Sally approaching the entrance to the tunnel.

'We're too late,' she shouted, as she saw them reach the tunnel and, stooping, disappear from sight. 'They've found it. We're too late. We can't stop them now.'

The wind of their speed tore the hopeless words from Jinny's mouth, for although the Walker had seen the two humans going into the tunnel they did not slacken their wild ride until they had reached the foot of the mound.

'At the tunnel mouth there is a stone balanced in the wall. When I remove it the tunnel will collapse, the cave shatter,' said the Walker. His voice, despite their galloping, was deep and harsh, without any trace of breathlessness.

Somewhere in the depths of Jinny's memory, she heard the words of Mrs Cluny, her history mistress, as she told her class how many of the Egyptian pyramids had been designed so that the disturbance of a stone, centuries after they were built, would collapse a tunnel within the pyramid killing the trespassers.

'But Royce and Sally!' gasped Jinny. 'They're inside the tunnel now.'

The green eyes of the Walker held Jinny in their intensity and she knew with a sick, cold horror what he intended to do. He would take away the balance stone, crashing tunnel and cave into ruins while Royce and Sally were still inside.

'You'd kill them,' screamed Jinny as the Walker moved towards the tunnel mouth. 'You can't. Don't be crazy. It would be murder. You can't even think of doing that.'

Jinny flung herself down from Shantih, dashed to the Walker's side. Grabbing his arm she felt the strange suppleness of his sleeve, the flint-hard bone beneath it.

'They're people. I know them. They're my friends.'

The Walker shook Jinny from him, sending her sprawling on to the ground. He turned, looking down at her where she had fallen, and Jinny felt the otherness about him, his weirdness. She knew that his service to the cave and the dancing horses meant more to him than any human life. He would kill

Royce and Sally without a second thought, hardly noticing what he did; as snow or fire on the moors killed thousands of life forms, casually, unconsciously.

'Leave them to their folly. You serve the Golden Horses.'

'No!' Jinny cried. 'No!'

She scuttled to her feet, darted past the Walker and burst into the tunnel. The powerful blare of a torch blinded her.

'It's Jinny,' said Royce's voice. 'Come on and see what you've found. Once you've really seen it you'll forget all that nonsense about keeping it to yourself.'

'It is fantastic,' enthused Sally, her voice alive, sweet, singing. 'Come and look.'

Jinny could hear the Walker at the tunnel entrance. There was no time to start and try to explain. Royce would not listen to her garbled account of the Walker. She had to get them all out of the tunnel at once.

Jinny opened her mouth and screamed at the pitch of her lungs.

'What the blazes!' exclaimed Royce.

'Get out!' Jinny yelled. 'The mound is collapsing. A great crack. It's opening. Get out! Get out! Or you'll be buried.'

'If this is one of your tricks,' said Royce. 'I'll . . .' But Sally had him by the hand, was tugging him along behind Jinny as she bolted for the open air.

In her desperation to get everyone out, Jinny didn't see the Walker at the tunnel entrance; didn't know that he waited until she was clear of the tunnel before his hands closed on the stone. She tore on down to where Shantih stood and began to urge her away.

'Now,' Royce demanded. 'Show us what all this hysteria is about.'

Jinny looked back fearfully over her shoulder. The mound showed no sign of movement.

'I can't see any crack in it,' Sally said. 'Are you sure?'

Then the whole mound stirred, as if it breathed out, expanded before it crashed inward. The vibrations from the implosion threw Jinny to the ground. She lay face into the grass, feeling the earth move like a living being.

When at last she raised her head, daring to look up again, the mound had completely vanished. Only a wide, flat circle of rough ground marked where it had once been. Within the circle the ground was unsettled, crumpled. At its circumference a bow wave of earth and small stones lay on top of the ground. In a few months' time there would be no way of telling that the mound which had stood there for thousands of years had ever existed.

Shantih waited beside Jinny, staring out over the moor, her gaze fixed on a black shadow that moved through the bracken and was gone.

Jinny stood up. She threw her arms round her horse's neck, pressed her face against Shantih and felt the hot, bitter tears streaming down her cheeks. The Golden Horses were lost, buried, destroyed. They would never dance again.

Even when the others got back on to their feet and tried to comfort her, Jinny could only turn her face away and go on crying.

'In shock,' said Royce. 'And no wonder. That was a damn near thing.'

'We would have been killed,' said Sally. 'If you hadn't come to warn us we'd have been in there when it collapsed.' Her face was drained of colour, her arms wrapped round herself as she stood staring at where the mound had been. 'We'd have been dead. Dead now. Finished. Don't cry, Jinny. Don't. It's all right now. Really it is.'

'Could have been the find of a lifetime,' said Royce. 'And now it's nothing but rubble. Makes you think. I shan't be interfering with it again, that is for sure.'

Jinny pulled herself up on to Shantih and, ignoring their attempts to make her wait for them, pushed her into a canter and had soon left them behind.

CHAPTER TWELVE

Jinny rode vaguely, blinded by tears. She knew that soon she would need to start and find her way back to the hotel; to think up answers to all the questions that would be waiting for her there. And then the trek back to Miss Tuke's.

But it was too soon for Jinny even to admit to herself that these things existed. She could think of nothing but the glory of the Golden Horses. How, only a few hours ago, they had drawn her into their dance; lifted her into a new, bright world where all beings – plants, animals, humans, the very walls of the cave – were lifted up for joy. And now the cave paintings had vanished forever. They were no more than broken fragments of stone, some marked with a few crude lines, all lost.

No matter how much Jinny told herself that it was not her fault, could not possibly be her fault, for the Walker had taken her to the cave; he had removed the stone that had sent tunnel and cave crashing into oblivion, she could not help feeling that somehow she was to blame. Why had the Walker taken her with him? The feeling of guilt dragged her down. Royce would not have found the cave if he had not seen Shantih.

'Oh Shantih,' said Jinny wearily. 'Why? Why did it have to happen? Why did Royce have to see you? Why?'

Suddenly Shantih froze to attention, and Jinny heard a shiver of sound, a whinnying call. Without hesitation Shantih plunged towards the sound. Jinny, grabbing handfuls of mane, was a helpless passenger.

The Walker waited for them, standing in the shadow of an overhanging rock, close to a lochan that lay like a quicksilver patch of sky in the heather. Shantih galloped straight to him. She stopped beside him, whickering her delight at the touch of his hand.

'It was time,' he said, the dry crack of his lips hardly moving. 'I did not know it would be so soon. I thought you would have been given another year to grow to a clearer understanding of the mystery. But that was not to be. Now you must prove yourself. The dance must no longer be hidden.'

'But it's gone!' cried Jinny. 'Smashed, destroyed. The cave's gone forever. If it wasn't to be hidden why didn't you let Royce tell everyone about it? Once he'd put it on television it wouldn't have been hidden any longer.'

'Then it would have been truly destroyed,' said the Walker. 'You were sent to witness the dance, to carry it with you and to let it be seen again. To give it new clothing.'

'What?' said Jinny, having no idea what the Walker meant. How could the dance be seen again when it was shattered? She couldn't tell anyone about it for she didn't know what it was. Only knew there *was* a dance.

'Listen,' commanded the Walker. 'Today, in your world, many are searching desperately for a better understanding of life. The Golden Horses have let you experience this. Now you must ride the fire horse and carry their gift of inner vision with you. Only you can do this.'

Jinny sat on Shantih without words. She wanted to shout at the pitch of her voice that she didn't know

138

what the Walker was talking about, that she didn't understand him. She wanted to shout, 'No! No! No!', to leave the strangeness behind her, have no more to do with it. But she could not. She was the strangeness. The Golden Horses danced in her mind's eye.

'Come down,' said the Walker, and Jinny slid to the ground. 'Now draw the Golden Horses.'

Jinny took her sketch pad and pencil from her pocket. She felt silence about her, deepening concentric circles, rings of brightness and at their centre herself, Shantih and the Walker. Her pencil moved over the paper and the heavy lines of the cave paintings grew there. On page after page the horses took life. Although she only had a pencil Jinny saw orange and scarlet and glowing yellows body out the pencil line. She drew on until the energy left her. Her hand, suddenly clumsy, dropped her pencil and pad. She blinked her way back into a gross world of form and shape.

The Walker held out his hands to Jinny, clasping hers and lifting her to her feet. Her sketch pad lay between them. His green eyes had lost their terror, his gaunt face its winter pall. Neither broken tramp, nor the Walker, nor form of the Water Horse, he stood a noonday ghost of black brilliance.

'Ride the fire horse to Finmory, take the paints Keziah left with you and ride to the Wilton. Jo Wilton is expecting you. The Golden Horses will go with you.'

When the Walker released her, he left the little statue of the Horse god in Jinny's left hand.

'Go well,' he said. 'We wait on you.'

Jinny leapt on to Shantih. Knowing clearly the way to the hotel she urged Shantih into a canter. When

139

she looked back the Walker was not to be seen, only spangling rings on the disturbed surface of the lochan danced in the sun.

'I'll tell them that I'm going straight back to Finmory,' Jinny thought. 'That I can't wait for them. I'll take my haversack and just go. Ride home as fast as I can, collect the paints and ride on to the Wilton.'

Nothing else mattered except to reach the Wilton and paint the Golden Horses. If she failed there was no one else who could do it. The shattered fragments of the paintings would never find new life.

As Jinny rode into the hotel grounds, towards the ponies' field, she suddenly remembered that there were eight Highland ponies to be taken home to Miss Tuke's. Petra and Brian would ride two of them, which still left six ponies to be led back. Jinny knew Petra would never manage to lead two ponies. She wondered if Sue or Brian could cope with leading three ponies.

'Need to leave my haversack behind,' Jinny thought. 'Can't risk being seen? But then she imagined the fuss there would be if she didn't let them know where she was. Petra would panic.

As Jinny hesitated, not knowing what to do, Petra and Brian came round the corner.

'Big deal!' exclaimed Petra. 'Where have you been? And just when you could have been of some use for once.'

'I only went out for a ride,' Jinny apologised. She couldn't be bothered starting to defend herself against Petra. Could hardly be bothered answering her. She had to get away. At once.

'Royce and Sally have been back for ages,' said Brian.

'Where have you been since you left them?' demanded Petra. 'I've been worried stiff.'

'Well, you didn't need to be. I can look after myself.'

'Royce didn't seem to think so. Wait until Mum and Dad hear about you going off on your own. I think it's mental the way you're always riding off by yourself.'

'If I'm always doing it they won't be bothered. They'll be quite used to it. *If* I'm always doing it. And what's more I'm going to do it again.'

'Now you are here, you'd better come and look at Beech,' went on Petra, not listening to Jinny. 'He's really lame. We couldn't see anything wrong with his leg but he doesn't look as if he could make it to Miss Tuke's.'

'I can't . . .' began Jinny.

'Sue's with him,' said Brian and led the way to the field.

'I don't have to go with them,' thought Jinny. 'But if Beech has hurt himself I'd better have a look.' And she groaned aloud. So simple just to ride to the Wilton. Should have been so simple. But it wasn't, it wasn't.

'Well, hurry up,' she said aloud, her voice sounding strained and irritable.

'Listen who's talking,' snapped Petra. 'When we've been hanging round waiting for you.'

Sue was standing outside the field holding Beech.

'It's his front leg,' she said. 'Near fore.'

Jinny dismounted, and Petra took Shantih's reins.

'Let's see him,' Jinny said, and Sue made Beech walk out. He was very lame. Jinny crouched down and ran her hands over his near foreleg. She thought, 'I shouldn't be here! Shouldn't be here! Got to get to

141

the Wilton,' but said, 'His knee does feel hot and a bit swollen.'

'I thought it could be his knee. Thought he might have been kicked but there doesn't seem to be any cut,' Sue agreed.

When Jinny stood up she saw to her dismay that Petra had taken Shantih into the field, unbridled her and turned her loose.

'Oh no! What did you go and do that for?' Jinny cried. 'I've got to ride her home.'

'Before anyone starts to go home we've got to decide what to do with Beech. No point in hanging on to Shantih.'

'If only Miss Tuke were here,' said Sue.

'Phone her,' said Brian.

'Jinny,' said Petra. 'You know her best. On you go and phone.'

For a second Jinny stood speechless. She wanted to shout at them all that she hadn't time. She had to ride to the Wilton at once. But there was no way she could start and try to explain. In a blind panic she swung round and raced towards the hotel. Realising that she had no money for the public phone she asked the girl at the reception desk if should could use the hotel phone, explaining that one of their ponies was lame and she had to speak to the trek leader.

'It'll be that Miss Tuke you want?' said the girl. 'Nasty accident she had poor soul.'

'Yes,' said Jinny, realising that the whole of the hotel probably knew everything about them.

The receptionist found the number and suggested that Jinny should make it a reverse charges call. Jinny agreed.

'Mad,' thought Jinny. 'I'm crazy, standing here

142

being polite. I shouldn't be here, I should be galloping back to Finmory by now.' The girl handed her the receiver.

'Royce!' exclaimed Miss Tuke's voice.

'No, Jinny. Beech is lame. It's his near foreleg.'

'His knee? Came down on it a year or two back. Still plays him up,' boomed Miss Tuke. 'But it doesn't matter. Been trying to make contact, so listen. I've spoken to the hotel boss man and it's OK for you to leave the ponies in the field. Except Bramble for Petra and McSporran for Brian. Understand? I'll send my box over tomorrow to collect the rest. OK? And you've to come home by the short route. No more mountaineering.'

'Fine,' said Jinny. 'Right.' And forgetting to ask Miss Tuke how she was, Jinny slammed the phone down and raced back to the others.

'So we can go AT ONCE,' she gasped, when she had finished giving them Miss Tuke's message.

'We've to say goodbye to Royce,' said Petra.

'Not me,' said Jinny.

'You,' stated Petra, and once again Jinny was walking back to the hotel.

Royce and Sally were sitting at a table in the hotel lounge drinking coffee.

'You've time for a quick cup,' Royce called. 'Message for you from Auntie Tuke. You've to leave the ponies behind.'

'We know,' said Petra, sitting down. 'Jinny phoned her.'

'Ah, Jinny did, did she?' said Royce, looking directly at Jinny. 'So you got back?'

'Yes,' said Jinny, wondering desperately what Royce and Sally had told the others.

'And could we have some sandwiches?' Petra said

to the waitress. 'They're for my sister. You see she hasn't had any breakfast.'

Jinny groaned inwardly. Her urgency to reach the Wilton raged in her mind, she could hardly sit still, frothed over with nerves. She put her hand on her sketch pad in her pocket. She felt as if it contained living creatures entrusted to her safe keeping and here she was sitting doing nothing. For a moment Jinny almost sprang to her feet, ready to dash back to Shantih. But stopped herself just in time. This was no way for her to take the Golden Horses to the Wilton. She was behaving like Petra, twittering, flapping. Jinny sat back in her chair. She took long slow breaths, calming herself.

Brian spread out the map, and Jinny saw that after about three miles the track they were to take split – left for Miss Tuke's, right for Finmory. She would ride with the others until the fork and then gallop on to Finmory by herself.

'Time you were on your way,' said Royce at last. 'Auntie Tuke will be clucking her head off worrying about you.'

Their chat had all been about filming. There had been no mention of the cave.

'Yes,' agreed Petra. 'We'd better go and get the ponies saddled. Are you ready, Jinny?'

'She won't be a minute,' Royce said, and Jinny knew that he wanted to speak to her without the others.

Left alone with Sally and Royce, Jinny munched industriously.

'Ease up,' said Royce. 'We didn't spill the beans about the cave. Only that we'd seen you out riding on Shantih, rather more than early in the morning. Mentioned that it wasn't too good a thing for you to be tearing about over strange moors on your own.'

144

'You didn't tell them about the cave,' echoed Jinny in amazement. 'So that's why they weren't going on about it.'

'Our secret?' said Royce. 'Least we can do for you, considering you saved our lives. But whatever it was you were up to, it might have been a good idea to have told someone else where you were going.'

'Thanks,' said Jinny, slowly realising that it meant there would be no danger of newspaper reporters getting wind of it. In a few weeks' time all trace of the cave's existence would be covered up by autumn's decay. Next spring not even Royce with his eye for a country would be able to find its ruin. The broken forms of the Golden Horses would sleep undisturbed.

'Thanks,' said Jinny again.

'I'm not such a pure-bred plastic rotter after all?' teased Royce.

'You're not too bad an old stick,' said Sally.

Jinny grinned at him, seeing him as a pleasant, blond-haired young man but nothing more.

'Come on, Miss Manders, how about a kiss before you go?'

'Jinny! Will you hurry,' said Petra's voice from the doorway. 'We're all ready.'

Jinny disentangled herself from Royce's hug, her mind set on the ride to Finmory.

'I'm coming,' she said to Petra and raced upstairs for her haversack.

Royce and Sally came down to see them safely on their way.

'I'll arrange with Auntie Tuke for you all to see a preview. About three months from now. And thank you, thank you, thank you for all your efforts,' said Royce as he waved goodbye.

Shantih's long-striding walk quickly outpaced the Highlands. Jinny let her stretch her neck, leaving her reins loose. They were riding along a wide track that circled the wilderness of moorland which they had trekked over to reach Calmun. Her sketch pad lay safely in her pocket, and secure in her mind's eye she carried the vision of the Golden Horses.

They reached the fork in the track about midday.

'Stop here and eat our picnic?' asked Sue.

'Oke,' agreed Brian, sliding down from McSporran. 'At least it will be worth stopping for, not like Lillybank's poached eggs.'

Jinny could hardly remember Lillybank. It all seemed to have happened so long ago.

'Reckon we'll be back at Miss Tuke's in another three hours,' Brian said when he had finished eating, and Jinny seized her chance.

'I'm going straight back to Finmory,' she said. 'There's no point in taking Shantih over to Miss Tuke's.'

'Of course you're not,' exclaimed Petra. 'We're all going to Miss Tuke's. Don't you want to see how she is?'

'You can tell me,' said Jinny. She did want to know. She wanted to ride back with the others and share the evening together round Miss Tuke's fire, telling her all about their trek to Calmun and the filming. Of course she wanted to see Miss Tuke but she had no choice. 'I'm going straight home,' she said.

'Oh Jinny, don't be so tiresome. You're coming with us.'

'No,' said Jinny. She pushed the paperbags that had contained her lunch into her haversack, swung it on to her shoulders and mounted Shantih.

'You're spoiling everything,' pleaded Sue. 'This is the best bit. The triumphant return. Come on, Jinny. Don't be so mean.'

But Jinny's only answer was to touch her legs against Shantih's sides, sending her on along the track to Finmory.

'Come back, Jinny,' Petra shouted. 'Jinny!'

'I'll need to get the paints first,' Jinny thought, hardly hearing her sister's voice. 'Then ride to the Wilton.'

Riding to the Wilton meant riding through Inverburgh's city streets. Jinny's stomach tightened at the thought. Once before she had ridden to the Wilton but then Sue and Pippen had been with her. This time she would have to manage alone.

'Don't think about it,' Jinny told herself. 'Think about arriving at the Wilton.'

Jinny reached Finmory in the late afternoon. She knew that she had to get the paints that were hidden in her room without her parents seeing her. If her mother saw her there would be no chance of Jinny being allowed to ride on to Inverburgh that night. Her mother would insist that she waited until the morning, and Jinny was terrified that that would be too late. She had to get to the Wilton tonight. Had to paint the Golden Horses as soon as she possibly could. Jinny didn't dare to think about them, in case it would take away their energy and when she came to paint them she would find there was nothing left to paint.

Jinny rode down to the shore, not wanting to risk riding past Mr MacKenzie's farm. He would have been sure to have stopped her, chiselling to find out what she was doing. The path from the shore to Finmory could only be seen from the top windows of the house. If any of her family were upstairs they would be certain to see her. It was a chance she had to take. She rode towards the stables, her spine prickling, not daring to look up, for to have looked up would have drawn her parents to the window.

'It's not for long,' Jinny told Shantih as she led her into her box, her hooves sounding like thunder in Jinny's ears. 'Only 'til I get the paints. Then on to the Wilton.'

Jinny took off Shantih's bridle, loosened her girth and gave her a feed of pony nuts. She knew Shantih had done more than enough for one day but she didn't seem tired. Although she buried her face in the manger devouring the nuts, her attention was all on Jinny. She was as alert as if she was just starting the day.

Jinny shut the box door and made her way towards the house, not crossing the grass as she usually did but keeping well in to the shelter of the hedge. The light was on in the kitchen. Jinny crept nearer and saw to her delight that her mother was cooking, her father sitting reading. There was no sign of Mike. She would go in by the front door, straight up the stairs to her room. With any luck they would never hear her.

Cautiously Jinny circled the house, climbed the front doorsteps and stood in front of the heavy wooden door. She eased it open and, with her heart thumping in her throat, she stepped into the house. The familiar hall was full of menace. The passage that led to the kitchen was dark and shadowy. Jinny could hear the dim murmur of her parent's voices. Right foot, left foot, she crossed the hall and began to climb the stairs.

She was halfway up when she heard the kitchen

door open, her father's voice saying that perhaps she'd left it in the pottery. Jinny froze – her hand gripping the bannister was fixed there, her legs would not move. In seconds her father would come along the corridor and discover her.

'Here it is,' said her mother's voice, and Jinny breathed again.

She heard the door close and knew she was safe, but it had been very close. She ran silently along the corridor and up the steep flight of steps that led to her room.

The box of paints was hidden in the back of a cupboard. Jinny lifted it out and crouched on the floor, opening it beneath the mural of the Red Horse. Under the power of Keziah, the old tinker woman, Jinny had repainted the mural. Using the larger of the two brushes she had painted the red bulk of the Horse, its black mane and tail. Last of all she had painted its yellow eye, and Keziah, using the finer of the two brushes, had touched red pupils into the yellow eyes.

When Keziah had died a few days later she had left the paints, brushes and a stone bowl to Jinny. The earthenware pots of paint had been resealed, the brushes cleaned. Tam, Keziah's nephew had told Jinny that she was to keep them until an old one came. Jinny had thought that he meant another tinker, but she had been wrong.

Quickly Jinny closed the box and packed it away in her haversack. She went downstairs, hearing the sound of her parents voices, still safely in the kitchen. She closed the door and fled back to Shantih.

'The Wilton,' Jinny told Shantih when she was riding back down to the shore. 'We're expected there. They're waiting for us.'

The Arab tossed her head, flirted her feet, cantering sideways. Light as a blown feather, she was ready to carry Jinny to the ends of the earth, and although Jinny had been riding all day she didn't feel at all tired. It was as if the Wilton was a magnet drawing them to it without any effort on their part.

Jinny had considered riding over the hills and rejoining the Inverburgh road but she had decided that it would be safer to stick to the road all the way. They came up from the shore, on to the road that led first to Glenbost and then on to the main Inverburgh road.

Shantih settled into a steady trot, her will set forward as if she knew where she was going. As they rode, the bracken, patched with autumn gold, lost its colour to the greying evening. It would be dark by the time they reached the Inverburgh road. The traffic would have its lights on. Normally Jinny would never have dreamt of riding Shantih along that stretch of road at night, but this journey was different. The drawings in her pocket beside the little statue were linked with Epona and Jo Wilton. Jinny rode along a way made safe for her coming.

Traffic roared past them. First the swathe of headlights then the clattering, crashing juggernauts; the whining speed of sports cars; family saloons that came too close behind Shantih and then were afraid to pass. Looking neither to right nor left Shantih trotted on.

In Inverburgh the traffic hedged them in. They waited for traffic-lights to change, closed in by cars. If Shantih had panicked, her iron-shod hooves would have smashed through car bonnets and headlamps. Drivers and their passengers stared up at Jinny. They could find no place for her in their scheme of living and chose to ignore her. The pavements were busy, but the constantly moving silhouettes, black against the electric glare of the shop windows, flowed on, hardly noticing the skinny girl on her Arab horse.

Jinny found her way to the side street where the Wilton Collection was housed. She turned Shantih into its security, dismounted, and walking at her head, led her down a street of elegant tenement buildings. They had dropped into a pool of silence. Even the noise of the traffic seemed to be blown away over the high rooftops.

Suddenly Jinny thought about the others. They would be at Miss Tuke's, sitting round her fire, telling Miss Tuke and the next week's trekkers about their adventures – how they had taken the wrong track over the moors; ridden through the Pass of the Horses half blinded by mist; of their perilous descent to Calmun, and about Royce and the filming. Even Miss Tuke's accident would have become something to be retold round a fire. For a long moment Jinny ached to be with them. Not to be caught up in this strange mystery but to be sitting with Sue and Brian and Petra, the firelight flickering on Miss Tuke's clustering rosettes, and Shantih grazing beside Pippen in the paddock. She would have told them all about the hip-bath full of poached eggs in Lillybank's kitchen.

Jinny put her hand into her pocket and felt her sketch pad and the hard nugget of the statue. Halfway along the street a door opened and Jo Wilton came down the steps to welcome them. Instantly all thoughts of Miss Tuke's cosy room vanished.

'I have a stable ready for her,' he said. 'This way.'

He led them through a close between the

tenements and round to the back of the buildings.

'There,' he said, switching on a light, so that Jinny could see a high-ceilinged, old-fashioned loosebox. A thick straw bed, built up at the sides of the box, plaited at the door, waited for Shantih. The metal rack on the wall was full of hay, there was an oak bucket filled with fresh water, and a rich feed of oats, bran, chop and sliced carrot waiting in the stone trough. The walls and rafters were fungused with cobwebs. It must have been years since the stable had last been used.

'She has carried you well,' Jo Wilton said, and his hands, caressing Shantih as Jinny took off her tack, were sympathetic, the hands of a wise horseman. 'Rest well here. You have earned it.'

They left Shantih with her muzzle deep in the whispering oats. Jo Wilton switched off the light, closed the box door and led Jinny back to the main doors of the Wilton. Jinny put Shantih's sweated tack down at the foot of the stairs and followed him up to the long corridor that led to where the statue of Epona waited for the return of the Horse god. The room had been rearranged since Jinny had last seen it. Some of the glass cases had been taken away. The white wall opposite the case containing Epona was empty, nothing in front of it, nothing on it. Jinny slipped the haversack off her back. She would paint the Golden Horses here, on this wall.

'Before I leave you,' said Jo Wilton, 'there is a stone bowl with the paints. If you could let me have it.'

Jinny opened the box of paints and gave him the bowl. She couldn't see what he put into it but when he lit the contents of the bowl Jinny smelt the sweet incense that had filled her room when she had helped Keziah repaint the Red Horse.

'I have left you everything you will need,' Jo Wilton said, standing in the doorway, a neat, self-effacing figure, a gentle man.

Left alone, Jinny stood self-consciously looking about her. She still felt that someone was watching her. She took off her jodh boots, placed them by the door beside her haversack, then she crossed to the glass case and, lifting the lid, set the statue of the Horse god back beside Epona. Not one but One. She waited, seeing them clearly, both as statues and as she had seen them above the Celtic altar – gigantic beings of power.

She took out her sketch pad and, very carefully, eased the pages containing her drawings of the Golden Horses free from the wire spiral which bound them together. One by one she laid them on the floor. When they were all spread out, Jinny sat in front of them, concentrating on them totally, completely, until nothing existed for her except their shapes. From time to time she reached out, moving them into a different pattern, rearranging them. At last she was satisfied. She sat on, felt them lift from the pages until there was no difference between herself and the drawings. With the sweet smell in her nostrils, Jinny held them living in her mind's eye. She was conscious of the coming of the Golden Horses, their power infusing her drawings with spirit.

Jinny stood up, crossed to a table beside the wall where Jo Wilton had left water, dishes, paint rags and knives; everything that Jinny might need. She opened the box of paints, carefully unsealed the earthenware jars, poured water into a glass and, picking up the larger brush, she gazed at the wall. Stood silent, motionless, until the horses rose out of its white surface. Then, climbing on and off a stool, Jinny gave their shapes a strong black outline. She worked without any hesitation, without any awareness of herself. Using orange, red and yellow paint she blocked in the shapes she had drawn, giving them substance.

When she had finished she stood back. The horses were as they had been in the cave but it was not enough. The pressure of creation tightened in Jinny's being. She shook her hair rapidly from side to side trying to escape. Not enough. Not finished. But she had drawn all she could. The wall was blazoned with the Golden Horses. She could do no more. As if she were struggling to wake from a nightmare Jinny fought to escape but could not. The tension in her would not relax. More. Not finished. More. From the corners of her eyes Jinny thought she caught glimpses of figures standing in the shadows of the room, watching her, willing her to go on. Insubstantial as air they stood waiting.

'What?' cried Jinny. 'What more?'

'They have come out of the cave,' answered the Walker's voice. 'Into the light. Give them eyes. Let them see.'

Jinny took the finer brush, dipped it into the red paint and touched eyes into each blind head.

She had finished. She sat down on the floor; saw the wall infused with the dance. No longer blind but knowing itself. The dance made conscious.

Jinny collapsed on the floor, fell into a shaft of sleep, deep sleep without dreams.

She woke to bright midday sun and Jo Wilton calling her name. Stiff from sleeping on the floor she stood up and without looking at her painting she went out of the room, shutting the door behind her.

154

Following Jo Wilton's voice, she found herself in the small flat he occupied.

When she had washed, Jinny sat down to scrambled eggs, freshly ground coffee and warm breakfast rolls. The clock on the sideboard said half-past twelve.

'Shantih!' Jinny exclaimed, jumping up in dismay. 'I'll need to see her first.'

'Sit down. She is perfectly content. I have seen to her. Also, I phoned your parents last night.'

'What did they say?' Jinny asked guiltily. Before it hadn't mattered, now it did.

'I only told them that you were here, that they had no need to worry, that you were quite safe.'

'Good job you did,' said Jinny. 'Probably have had the police out by now.'

'Did it go well?' Jo Wilton asked.

Jinny knew from the tone of his voice that he meant her painting.

She nodded. 'Yes,' she said and went on gulping hot coffee, greedily eating egg and roll. The night had slipped away from her, its details forgotten. She could only remember its quality of joy. She had painted the Golden Horses, had brought them safely from the cave and given them sight. And for a moment, when she had finished painting them, they had danced again, opening the closed world as if it were a rose unfolding.

Suddenly Jinny couldn't wait to get back to see them again. She could hardly wait to finish her meal. That the Golden Horses were in the same building as herself, and she wasn't with them, seemed the most ludicrous thing. She had to see them at once. Be with them. Now they were secure in the sanctuary of the Wilton, other people would see them, not a television image of them or a labelled archaeologist's reduction, but as living beings. People would come and know the dance for themselves.

'Shall we go now and see them?' Jinny demanded.

'Easy,' said Jo Wilton. 'There is plenty of time. Finish your food.'

But even when they had finished eating, Jo Wilton insisted that they should wash their dishes before they went to look at the painting.

'As if he doesn't want me to see it again,' Jinny thought. 'As if he knows something I don't know.'

With meticulous care Jo Wilton slid the dishes through soapy water, through clear water, inspecting them minutely before he gave them to Jinny to dry.

'Oh hurry up! Hurry up!' cried Jinny silently. She couldn't bear his slowness, couldn't listen to him talking about his collection. Jinny didn't care about it. She only wanted to be back where the dance of the Golden Horses waited to catch her up and carry her to its new land.

At last they had finished – sink wiped down, tea towel hung up to dry. Running impatiently ahead of Jo Wilton, Jinny sped back to her painting.

'Look,' she cried, throwing open the door, urging him in.

The table was littered with emptied jars of paint, unwashed brushes, jars of dirty water and smeared painting rags. On the floor lay the pages of her sketch pad, scattered about, scuffed and soiled.

A cold shudder of dread laid icy fingers on Jinny. She looked up at the wall but there was no magic dance. Only a flat painting without life; a copy of drawings from a Stone Age cave. Nothing more than a mural painted to decorate a room.

The ice cold bit into Jinny's bones, tightened on

her heart and mind. It had all been a nonsense. She stood clenched tight and desolate. She could not hear Jo Wilton praising her work.

'But it's no use,' she cried. 'There's nothing there. Only a stupid painting. Nothing, nothing at all. Last night it was alive. I thought . . .'

'That you could paint the dance?' Jo Wilton's voice was warm with understanding, yet edged with mockery.

'They were something else,' cried Jinny, her misery forcing her to try to tell Jo Wilton how it had been. 'It was all new and now there's nothing. Nothing of how it was for me. That's what I wanted to paint.'

'That's what we all want to paint,' Jo Wilton said. 'That's why we keep on trying; why we go ourselves into the golden land, experience it, know it and come back, trying to tell others how it is. We can do no more. Experience it, come back and try to make a mark to point the way.'

'Last night I thought I had brought the dance from the cave.'

'You did.'

'I wanted other people to know about it. Not messed up the way it would have been if they'd got into the cave and spoilt it, but to know the real thing.'

'They will. That was what they wanted, the old ones who painted the cave. It was time for the Golden Horses to leave the cave. They have eyes now. They can see. They will find a way.'

Wearily Jinny began to tidy up. She wanted to be back with Shantih, to be back at Finmory.

'You have done well,' Jo Wilton said, as he stood at Shantih's head while Jinny mounted. 'It will never

157

be easy. Never be how you think it should be. Be content.'

'Bye,' said Jinny, shallow and quick, as she tugged at Shantih's girth. She wanted to get away as soon as she could; to leave it all behind her. 'Bye.'

She rode into the Inverburgh traffic, felt Shantih ready to spook and shy. A double-decker bus loomed beside them, and Shantih flung herself away from it, her shoes scoring the road. A mother shook her shopping bag at them, defending her child, and Shantih plunged towards the bus again.

Sitting hard down in her saddle, pushing Shantih into her bit, Jinny drove her forward. The urgency of getting Shantih through Inverburgh took up the whole of Jinny's attention. With plunging half-rears Shantih bounded along the city streets. Goggle eyes, tip-touching ears proclaimed that she had never experienced such horrors in her life before.

Once clear of Inverburgh, Shantih raced for Finmory. Her trot was raking, unbalanced, out of control. Jinny, tugging at her reins, was jolted up and down by her speed. At last Jinny saw the place ahead of her where a track led over the hills, directly to Glenbost. She turned Shantih off the road and with an enormous buck Shantih burst into a gallop. Knowing there was no point in trying to fight her, Jinny let her gallop on.

The sky was bright about them, bracken and reeds patched with gaudy colour, and Shantih was real, strong and true. Jinny shook her head, clearing her mind of the drifting miasma of the past few days – the strange, haunting presence of the Walker; the spirit of the cave; the trust the Golden Horses had laid upon her; Jo Wilton knowing so much more than she did, and her bleak dismay when she had returned

158

to find her painting was such an ordinary thing. Jinny rode to leave it all behind her; galloping Shantih at a stone wall, she wanted no more of them. As Shantih leapt, soared over the wall, touched down to gallop on, Jinny wanted nothing but the freedom of her galloping horse.

They climbed over the ridge of the hills and dropped down to Glenbost. Jinny was thinking about Royce, remembering the boredom of filming, wondering how Miss Tuke was, thinking that she would ride over to see her before she went back to school. School! And with the thought of school came the realisation that the holidays were almost over. The Hortons would be going home tomorrow. Her holiday with Sue that she had looked forward to for so long was over. It had never happened.

Settling into her everyday world Jinny rode through Glenbost and on to Finmory. There was no one about. She gave Shantih a feed of pony-nuts and stood leaning over the box door watching her horse eating – loving Shantih so much that at moments like this it hurt. She loved her strength and gaiety; the brittle quality of her bones beneath her satin skin; the packed muscle at shoulder and quarter. Shantih turned to look at Jinny, the long hairs on her muzzle dusty with shreds of pony-nuts, her lips clown-green with froth.

'Dear Shantih,' said Jinny laughing.

With her laughter came the inner touch, the flicker of consciousness. And Jinny knew that she could not try to pretend that what had happened had been no more than a nonsense. She could not put it behind her. It had been real. As real as Shantih. Whatever this secret otherness, it could not be dismissed by a gallop over the hills. Shantih had known it too. She had been as much a part of the mystery as the Walker or Jinny herself.

Jinny opened the box door, and with her arm over Shantih's withers, they walked down to the field together. Jinny opened the gate and Shantih trotted in. She stood for a second, her head high, testing the air, then, swinging her head, scattering her mane, she surged into an explosion of bucking. Round and round the field she went, head down, hind feet hammering the sky. The sun broke from behind the clouds, and for a second Shantih was held in a ray of sunlight. For a dazzling moment she danced with the Golden Horses.

Watching, Jinny gasped aloud, for of course the dance was here and now. She had not left it behind in the ruins of the cave, nor was it confined to the walls of the Wilton. The dance was everywhere. You had only to open your eyes to see it.